Introduction

At this point it is apparently u
thanks to all those who have
extravaganza possible.

Thus I tender my grateful thanks to my lady wife and three daughters who have put up with me for a number of years.

Also I suppose I ought to explain why I have ventured into the novel format. The answer is very simple and falls into two parts.

The first is that some stories take longer to tell, and thus the shorter novella format (which I love) is not necessarily the best vehicle.

The second is that a novel takes twice as long to read, thus ensuring I have an even larger head start when people finally get to the end of the story. These little details can be vitally important at times.

To Bishop James

With all Best
Wishes

Chapter 1

It has to be confessed that the explosion was spectacular. What made it even more spectacular was that it happened in the Sump, which is the lowest point of the city, thus a lot of people saw it. I am acquainted with a perfectly respectable matron who claimed she saw an entire roof rise vertically into the air before closing like a book and collapsing back down into the ruins. The fact that I know the lady was in Prae Ducis at the time rather discredits her as a witness, but still. The explosion was 'an event.' Everybody claimed they remembered exactly what they were doing when it happened. Everybody except Wodrik Artel. Wodrik was an alchemist. Some of them rather shun that term nowadays, preferring to be called 'natural philosophers' or even 'manipulators of the aether.' The latter term I feel reeks of pretentiousness and whenever I hear it I wonder what they are trying to compensate for.
Still the tale of the late Wodrik Artel is interesting, only in that it is connected in some small way to the story I hope to tell. He was in the habit of tinkering with those things man was not meant to know. His wife had, after several unfortunate accidents that needed three maids and a joiner to clean up after, banned him from experimenting in the house. Thus he was forced to hire a workroom some distance from his abode. This shows how far he had fallen. Even necromancers manage to have a workroom in their own home. Admittedly few of them have wives, but still, I feel the point still stands.
Now it just so happens that the Shrine to Aea in her Aspect as the Personification of Tempered Enthusiasm happened to own a small property in the Sump.
In all candour it was something of a burden as it wasn't really habitable.

We'd been left it by a widow who bequeathed several contiguous properties in the area to the order of Aea in all her Aspects, with the instruction that one of them should be signed over to our shrine in perpetuity.

The order looked at its new asset and decided that, frankly, demolition and rebuilding was the way forward. Under the sharp eye of Archhierophant Battass Droom, this was done. It was suggested to us that we included our property in the scheme, but frankly we hadn't the money. Also there was a sneaking suspicion that we'd end up with less property at the end of the process than we had when we started. So we declined to take part with every appearance of regret.

Not long after, Wodrik approached us. Our property was perfect for his purposes, it just about kept the rain out and nobody minded if he did a little superficial damage. So he worked away happily for some months. He was oblivious to the building work next door, and went back to his own home every evening. I suppose in retrospect we should have worried that he was indeed so engrossed in his project but I'm not sure any of us would have been any the wiser had we seen what he was doing. He had splashed oil of vitriol onto iron filings and noticed a fizzing. It struck him that a gas must be given off so tried to collect the gas. Initially he did this by having a paper cone over the vessel producing the gas, but the gas had the power to lift the paper. This intrigued him and he experimented by using larger quantities of reagents and a larger paper cone of daintier paper. Now you must remember, during this period, Maljie had made ballooning fashionable amongst a certain set. I would categorise them as the young, wealthy, and mad. This may be harsh, because many of those with only the feeblest grasp on sanity are still sane enough to avoid flight. It appeared to be those who were fascinated by mechanical contrivances who succumbed to this malaise.

It seems that Wodrik felt that if he could trap enough of this gas he could power a balloon without all that nonsense of burners, flames, hot air and fragile fabric envelopes.

With Wodrik, to think was to act. He purchased a balloon envelope second-hand from Maljie. To be fair she taught him the techniques of sealing it to keep gas it. Then by the simple expedient of removing the internal floors, he erected his canopy within the house. How he intended to remove it once full I'm not entirely sure. It may be that he rather suspected his plan wouldn't work. It might even be that he'd never considered it. Or of course he might just have intended to make a hole in the roof large enough to have the balloon leave through. In all candour this is the sort of thing that even the most casual landlord seeks to discourage in their tenants.

It must be said the technical details of what he was trying to achieve were enough to overwhelm a lesser, or at least a saner, man. Obviously mixing chemicals in a crucible was never going to fill his balloon canopy. Nobody had ever done things at this scale before. He had been producing his oil of vitriol by burning sulphur and saltpetre together in the presence of steam. Apparently oil of vitriol condensed on the glass vessel and he collected it in a tank.

Now as you can imagine, burning these two substances together produces an unfortunate odour. Wodrik took to working at night when there were fewer people about. Perhaps coincidentally, there was something of a religious revival in the area as people claimed to have dreamed of being cast into one of the less pleasant hells for their sins. Eventually he produced half a ton of his oil of vitriol and arranged to pour it onto a ton of scrap iron.

The vessel holding this mixture was below the mouth of the balloon and Wodrik was gratified at how quickly his balloon seemed to inflate.

Indeed the general feeling is that if he hadn't lit a celebratory pipe of lichen, his experiment would have been a complete success. Alas, the first sparks from his match must have produced the explosion.

📖📖📖

When the rain of rubble diminished the survivors crept out from their homes and surveyed the scene. Our property had disappeared entirely. There was merely a mound of debris. A demolition contractor would have struggled to match Wodrik for completeness. Unfortunately neighbouring buildings had also suffered. This is the Sump after all, maintenance is never a priority and any work done is rarely better than slipshod. So our property was surrounded by a circle of buildings that were either demolished or so badly damaged they would have to be demolished. It was rather embarrassing that the new building the Archhierophant Battass Droom had erected using the order's money had suffered more than most.

Apparently the order investigated the matter, holding an inquiry. Droom explained that the order's property had regrettably taken the worst of the blast thus taking the worst of the damage.

As somebody who also surveyed the scene of destruction, I for one was unimpressed by the quality of timber used, and the mortar struck me as distinctly inferior. Still, I was shown the financial accounts of the project, and the order had certainly paid for good quality materials.

Still, scapegoats were needed. Wodrik was assumed to be deceased. All that anybody found were his boots. To be fair, this is the Sump. Had his boots not still had his feet in them, they too would probably have disappeared. The order, rather unfairly, turned on us.

Fortunately our defence was sound.

The incumbent pointed out that Wodrik had signed the standard tenancy agreement. Whilst it doesn't explicitly enjoin a tenant not to destroy the property and neighbouring properties in tremendous explosions, it does specifically state that the tenant is forbidden to do anything which may damage the fabric of the building or adjacent buildings.

The eye of Battass Droom then fell on Maljie. After all, as he saw it, she had assisted, even encouraged Wodrik in his madcap schemes by providing him with a balloon envelope. Here, Maljie, when questioned by the incumbent at the formal hearing, admitted she had provided the envelope but pointed out that in her many years of experience with balloons, none of them had ever exploded. She was willing to agree that fire was a risk, but she had warned him about this, and as the record showed, there was very little fire damage. Such as there was had occurred in circumstances consistent with candles or lanterns being knocked over as a result of the explosion. Eventually those conducting the hearing, a bench of leading Sinecurists, handed down their formal opinion. The whole thing was an unfortunate accident and they felt no blame could be attached to anybody. They did mention that the city should consider a presumption against folk tampering with the forces of nature within the boundaries of the city, but this wasn't taken forward by the Council of Sinecurists who agreed that having houses explode hadn't been a problem previously and they felt it was unlikely to become a regular occurrence in the future. Still they agreed that a 'watching brief' was probably wise.

We retired back to the shrine feeling vindicated, Archhierophant Battass Droom on the other hand obviously felt aggrieved. It is unfortunate that he was not one of those who can accept the lesson and learn from it. Perhaps it was fending off difficult, nay, embarrassing questions about the quality of the work he had overseen that soured him against us.

Perhaps he is just somebody who is naturally vindictive. For whatever reason, in our eyes he was obviously was just watching for a chance to 'clip our wings.'

Chapter 2

It must be admitted that within every profession, craft, or trade there are those who fail to shine. At the same time there are those who stand head and shoulders above their peers. So if you were to go into the upstairs bar of the Misanthropes Hall and ask the poetasters gathered there to name the three greatest poets of the current generation, you'd probably come away with five names.

Upon reflection, you would be wise to pass quietly from table to table doing your survey. Standing on the bar to attract attention and asking the assembled company as a group is merely asking for a brawl. Similarly, you would have to ask the question. If I attempted it, they would leave my name off merely to be aggravating.

On the other hand, you'll find, when you sift through the generality of humanity, it is rare to find a person who doesn't display some competence in at least one area. With the order of Aea in all her Aspects there are many people with a wide array of gifts. Yes we find people with the skills one might expect, but there are other, unexpected areas of genius. I have found several with an obvious talent for obfuscation. In others I have seen futile ineffectuality taken to unexpected heights of excellence. Finally if you want to discover the masters of the art of procrastination, they seem to congregate in the Office of the Combined Hierophants of Aea.

One advantage accrues to an organisation which treasures these skills. Change is slow, measured and far from inexorable.

These folk can be likened to the weed clinging to the hull of a sailing ship that is in need of careening. They slow it down and stop the institution making those mistakes caused by an unhealthy enthusiasm for haste and innovation.

But within that forest of clogging weed there are predators. Some sit like stones, unmoving, trapping those unwary enough to venture into their vicinity. Others slip through the weed like voracious fish, long, lean, and many fanged. They use the weed as cover for their activities. It had occurred to me sometime previously that the Archhierophant Battass Droom fell into this latter category. Now whilst I do not socialise with the higher echelons of the order, it so happens that professionally I hear quite a lot about some of them. Obviously Archhierophants and their like are unlikely to hold the sort of entertainments for which the enlightened hire a poet. They are unlikely to attend such amusements. But they will have mothers, siblings or other family members who do. Let us not beat about the bush here, I hear the gossip. The sister of a minor incumbent would mention to her friends, her voice resonant with increasing indignation, that her brother was being pressured into signing over a small plot of land that had been left to his shrine a generation or more back. He used it as a play area for children. Alas, but somebody in the hierarchy has spotted the site's value should one wish to build a desirable residence. Or even to add it to your already extensive garden.

Or a proud mother would whisper that her son's success in the building trade began when he came to an 'arrangement' with a senior cleric to provide all those construction materials needed by the order, for a 'consideration'.

Now I do not wish to intimate that the order is corrupt, far from it. But the nature of institutions is that the corrupt can find niches within them in which they can flourish.

Still looking more positively, the order does manage to make some use of the more worthwhile skills members have. Thus one incumbent was, in his youth, a prize fighter. His small temple is considered by many to be a shrine to that art, and many young people have been saved from worse fates by their love of the pugilistic arts. Our city has many rough and violent young people, but thanks to him a proportion of them are competently rough and violent, and also decent young people. Another incumbent was a jockey in her youth, and her connections with the race course have provided a route to work for some young people. It must also be admitted that her establishment is largely funded by the money she has taken from the bookmakers, both as winnings, and also as they pay out to salve their consciences.

In our case, our incumbent is known both for preaching, but also for her ability to pour oil on troubled waters and to help people let bygones be bygones. Given the forceful actions of her temple wardens over recent years it may be that this latter skill is one she has been forced to learn 'on the job.' But still we see a lot of very junior members of the order come to her to improve their preaching. They'll arrive with their sermon text and she will take them through it. Once the heretical or merely wrong has been eliminated she will gather a congregation of mendicants who will listen to the preacher. This done, she will then lead the apprentice preacher through the mistakes and errors of delivery and point out where things could be improved. The new and improved sermon will then be delivered to the mendicants who will again listen attentively. Finally our incumbent will ask the novice to point out weaknesses that occurred to them.

Together they will work on the text one more time until finally, with increased confidence, the sermon is once more delivered.

Admittedly the mendicants hear it three times, but after all, 'Repetition is the key to mastery'. Also as one of the mendicants commented to me, "It's wet outside, and this is an indoor job with no heavy lifting.' As a side effect we do have some unusually theologically well informed mendicants. Across the order as a whole, it is not unusual for a proportion of mendicants to take the various vows and advance within the order. In the case of our shrine the number coming forward is usually high. Personally I put this down to self-defence on their part. After a certain point the victim realises that it is probably better to be the one at the front inflicting the sermon than the one in the seat, squirming.

Still you can understand that it is not unusual for our incumbent to be asked to give a day or so to some other temple, helping them whip their minor preachers into shape. What was unusual was when our incumbent was contacted from a monastery up in the Northern Aphices Mountains. The Shrine of Aea in the Wilderness is well thought of. I'd actually met the abbot, or hegumen, Sydna. He is one of those men whom everybody instinctively recognises as a genuinely spiritual person. I'm not sure I've met anybody who in my brief acquaintance struck me as so unworldly. Small children will spontaneously climb onto his lap; he speaks and even poets shut up and listen. He can command a room without raising his voice. On the other hand he does give the impression of a man who has little grasp of the realities of the world. I suspect that the only reason his monastery keeps running is due to the competence of his Claustral Prior.

One of the traditions Sydna introduced to his monastery is that all the monks take turns to read and preach to all the other monks as they eat, or work in various indoor activities. Somebody had commented unfavourably about the quality of preaching and the Hegumen Sydna contacted the Office of the Combined Hierophants of Aea.

Much to his surprise, he received a response within three months and even more surprising the response was relevant and helpful. He was advised to contact us.

When faced with this plea, given that it was summer, the weather was fine and the mountains beautiful, our incumbent decided she ought to go. Now you might ask yourself how we manage without an incumbent. In day to day matters things can tick over nicely. Indeed they can tick over better than nicely because there is one less person in authority asking difficult questions or pointedly glaring at the mendicant who missed their bath. So we were confident that we could ensure matters ran smoothly and we wouldn't have any serious problems. The system is one we have practiced over the years. Maljie and Laxey go round some of our more troublesome neighbours, intimating that now is not a good time to try our patience. We also rope in a few elderly priests who have hardly any duties and who are happy enough to drop by and tackle those tasks that fall to ordained. Some always comment how good it is to get back into harness for a little while. Indeed they preach with confidence because none of us remember their favourite sermons that they'd inflicted too often on a previous generation.

So we were a little surprised when the incumbent summoned us all to meet the Deacon, a member of the Idiosyncratic Diaconate. Apparently he'd just been ordained and was looking for a position, so she took him in to be part of the team.

Somewhat tentatively, Laxey asked what we needed a deacon for.

The incumbent produced a sheaf of notes and flicked through them. "We are quite successful finding work for our younger mendicants."

Maljie nodded at this. She is justly proud of our record.

The incumbent continued, "Over the past three years we've had thirty-seven taken on by usurers."

That I could understand. With Maljie and her connections we'd been able to do a lot of good. "Of the thirty-seven, eleven have been taken on as clerks, one as a cleaner, and the rest as enforcers." The incumbent put away her notes. "I rather feel that we needed to offer a wider range of skills. Our deacon, being the Lector, will be ideally placed to give both theological training as well as more practical training. This will hopefully help us improve on an already good position."

Our deacon or lector had arrived pushing a handcart. On it was a small bag of clothes, a somewhat larger bag of theological tomes, and a very large chest. The latter we discovered later contained carpentry tools. By the time he arrived, the various bags were hidden under 'useful bits of wood that are bound to come in.'

Now it so happened that our relatively newly appointed ostiary had taken himself off to advance his education. The suspicion was that he would return as a theologian, a cook, or as one of those who advises usurers as to how they ought to estimate the possible return on their potential investments. The smart money was on the latter. Still his room was now available. Admittedly it was little more than an empty cell, separated from the world by a curtain rather than a door. As befits a doorkeeper's cell it was right by the main door and Laxey had been coveting it as an office.

We all gathered to wave our Incumbent off. Indeed we took special care to make sure that the shrine looked well, the mendicants were thoroughly scrubbed and various known trouble makers, both lay and ordained, were mysteriously absent. As Maljie commented, "An old temple warden told me to make sure that if your incumbent has to travel, the last view of their shrine is a positive one. You want to tempt them back, not encourage them to keep going."

There was some concern as to how long our incumbent could be missing. It was estimated to take at least three weeks to get there, perhaps four, and by definition the same to get back. Also we assumed that she'd stay there for at least a month. So it would be autumn before we got her back. Indeed as she left she commented that it would be delightful to travel home through the autumnal woodlands and enjoy the colours of the season. Obviously there was a sense of holiday in the air. Still, when all's said and done, we faced the summer with quiet confidence. This may have been misplaced.

　　　　　　📖📖📖

It could have been three weeks later when I was out and about early. I crossed the open area in front of the shrine just as dawn was breaking. In reality I was just distressingly late rather than early. A patron had organised an evening entertainment. I had been asked to perform but had not been asked to do anything else. Thus after the first hour I had been forced to make various suggestions to her as she tried to restore order. By midnight I was effectively in charge and it took us three hours to disperse the guests. To be fair to the guests it was not their fault. It was purely because somebody had taken punch and cake to the sedan chair bearers. Obviously at any event you have to make provision for those who come in their own chair. I know some hostesses who insist that the bearers remain outside the gate, but frankly this is a recipe for disaster. It is far better to bring them into a room near the kitchen, give them meat pies and a bottle or two of beer each and leave them to talk or snooze as their fancy takes them.
I suppose punch and cake is not an entirely bad idea, but somebody had taken it upon themselves to substitute pure spirit for at least half the wine.

Most of the chair-men could barely stand, never mind walk carrying a chair. We were having to organise carts to get the sedan chairs and their bearers home, as well as trying to hire fresh chairs to get the guests home.

By the time everybody had departed and I felt it was safe to abandon my patron to the charms of her own bed, the false dawn hung in the east. Still, accentuating the positive, she had been suitably grateful, and had not merely thanked me effusively, but had given me a bag of assorted cold cuts to take home. When she thought I was not looking, she slid three bottles of the offending punch into my bag. I assume this was to ensure there was no evidence available during the inevitable family post mortem later that day. Thus in spite of the hour I was in a good humour and at ease with the world.

It was as I passed through Exegesis Square that I became aware of three men working on the area of open ground in front of the shrine. I stopped to watch and it was apparent that they were surveying the area. I confess I was rather surprised by this and drifted across to join them. Two were obviously assistants, their task was to hold poles or the end of tape measures. The third was by his actions the one in charge. He stood at the plane table and told the other two what to do. Eventually he told his two minions to 'stand down' and they came and joined me on the only bench. I pulled out one of the bottles of punch, took a sip and passed it to the minion next to me. He took quite a deep draught, coughed, and passed the bottle to his companion. A little hoarsely he commented, "It's not without authority."

His companion, forewarned, drank more carefully. "You can taste the fruit."

He passed the bottle back to me. I asked, "Surveying?"

"Yes," said the first man, who'd regained full control of his vocal cords. I took another sip, passed him the bottle and asked, "What for?"

He drank deep and then passed the bottle to his companion. "You know, once you get used to it, it's quite good stuff." He paused and shouted to the one in charge. "Who're we surveying this for?"

That gentleman came across, intercepted the bottle and tried some. "You're right, it is good stuff. But yes, we do the surveying for the Office of the Combined Hierophants of Aea. There's been a lot of talk about senior clergy being out of touch with their congregations. So they're going to give each archhierophant their own shrine to look after."

I asked, "Who does whatever archhierophants normally do, if they're looking after a shrine?"

"I think the idea is that they give them a small shrine where there's not a lot of work, and they'll probably just handle the important stuff, leaving the work to sub-hierodeacons and other suchlike undesirables."

I nodded wisely and as the first bottle was almost empty, opened the second. "But why the surveying?"

"Oh that's because they'll have to build a suitable residence for whoever gets the position."

"But the incumbent has a residence."

The surveyor shrugged. "That'll probably just be assigned to somebody's mistress. Either that or they'll rent it out."

One of his minions took the new bottle, drank deeply, and commented, "That's the way of it nowadays. Somebody comes up with a new bright idea about how the various shrines and temples are run and suddenly everything's kicked up into the air again."

"Who came up with this bright idea then?"

The two minions looked at the surveyor, one of them said, "Isn't it Archhierophant Droom who's in charge."

The surveyor reached for the bottle. "Yes, apparently this shrine is going to be a test case. He told a meeting of the Combined Hierophants that he felt that as it was his reform, he ought to be the experimental subject. So he'll be in charge and living here."

Chapter 3

Now a lesser man might have panicked. I, on the other hand, decided to go home to bed. As it was, I boarded the barge half an hour before Shena, my lady wife, left to catch the tide. Soon her shore comber clients would be coming to her office with items they hoped she, as a mud jobber, would buy from them.

It was gone noon when I finally breakfasted on cold roast mott and pondered the situation. As an aside some wives go through their husband's pockets looking for money or evidence of illicit liaisons. If I arrive home late, Shena will check my coat next morning on the off chance I've got something for breakfast.

Still, back to the tale I'm telling. You must understand that the position of incumbent at the Shrine of Aea in her Aspect as the Personification of Tempered Enthusiasm is unusual. In most shrines the Office of the Combined Hierophants of Aea merely chose an appropriate candidate, after taking advice from the hierophant of the appropriate aspect. Indeed, to be more accurate, they will tend to just rubber-stamp the hierophant's suggestion. But at our shrine, because of its proximity to the Sinecurists' Stair, and also because of our informal connection with the sinecurists as a group, the position is in the joint gift of the Council of Sinecurists and the Autocephalous Patriarch. So how was Battass Droom pushing our incumbent out? After finishing my coffee I made my way to the shrine, I felt that others needed to know of my discovery.

📖📖📖

It was a grim faced collection who heard my tale. Maljie, as senior temple-warden took the chair with our deacon sitting next to her.

Old Prophet Weden was present, Laxey in his capacity as sub-hierodeacon was there, along with a number of the more reliable mendicants. I had opened my final bottle of punch, I felt that we needed the clarity it must surely bring.

After I finished my tale, there was some discussion. A muttered suggestion that Battass Droom ought to trip over his shoelaces into the path of a runaway coach and four was dismissed as unworthy of us. At least for the time being. Various options were considered, and eventually Maljie summed up the matter succinctly. "We have to find out what is going on. Laxey, go and talk to people in the Office of the Combined Hierophants."

"It's always useful to have a reason in case some officious doorman asks what I'm doing."

"Just tell them that they've got our deaths register for reconciling. We need it back."

One of the mendicants said, "But the register is in the incumbent's office."

"They don't know that. They'll look round, assume they've lost it and at that point they'll go awfully quiet and stop talking to us."

Laxey gestured to me, "I'll get Tallis to write a receipt for us, and he can hand that in whilst I talk to people."

Now there is an art of producing a receipt in these circumstances. Firstly the person who issued the receipt has to be grand enough for clerks in the various offices to feel they do not wish to bother them with details.

There again the person has to be someone who might convincingly have visited our shrine. Thus it is possible that the incumbent smiled at them and said, "As you're passing, could you drop our deaths register into the office for reconciling."

Finally we need a specimen of their handwriting.

To give an extreme example, we have in our shrine plenty of examples of the Autocephalous Patriarch's signature.

Also I can well imagine that the clerks would hesitate to bother him with trivia. But there again, even I struggle to produce convincing reasons for him dropping in to see us.

At the opposite end we have 'Giggles' Bottichuck. He is, improbably, an Archhierophant, although you would never guess it. We see him on a regular basis as he has some vague responsibility for mendicants, and they look forward to his visits. He is cheerful, avuncular, and generally good to deal with. For old 'Giggles' nothing is too much trouble. The problem is that the clerks would have no hesitation turning up at his office and presenting him with the receipt.

The obvious choice was Battass Droom. He was always poking his nose into things, so he could well have been here. We have plenty of documentation with his annotations in the margins, and nobody in their right mind would draw his attention to them. Thus is was that on the appropriate, if yellowing, stationery, I drew up an appropriate receipt in a fair approximation of Archhierophant Droom's hand. I scrawled his signature at the bottom, blotted it carefully and pronounced myself ready. Laxey and I then sallied forth.

The Office of the Combined Hierophants of Aea is a rambling building. Initially a private house on one of the streets behind Ropewalk, as the bureaucracy expanded, other houses were purchased as they became available. Now there were three houses, but they weren't contiguous, there was still one house in the middle of the block occupied by a cantankerous widow. Denying the Combined order a chance to purchase her house to ease their situation had given her a reason for living. People expected her to see out her century.

We entered the main door, and by waving the receipt I mollified the guardian and he graciously allowed us to pass. I made my way down one corridor whilst Laxey took the stairs.

In the registry, I produced the receipt and waited politely whilst two increasingly worried clerks hunted for our register. Eventually they promised to search the document archive to ensure it hadn't been misfiled. Ever courteous I thanked them for their efforts. They suggested I leave the receipt so that they had it to help with their search. Let us not beat about the bush, I may be a poet and unworldly but I am not that unworldly. The receipt would have rapidly disappeared leaving no evidence that we had not lost our register. I smiled pathetically and pointed out that they could have it with my blessing, but obviously, Maljie would expect a receipt for the receipt. The clerk behind the counter paled a little at this but grimly wrote me out a receipt. Now armed against the vicissitudes of fate with a genuine receipt, I bowed my way out of their drab sanctum. I then followed Laxey's route up the stairs.

Now in every organisation that in any way manages to keep running, there has to be a cadre of competent and efficient people. To an extent they tend to know each other and form a web which holds things together. Laxey was simply visiting the office that was the heart of this web. I knocked on the door and entered the office. Immediately I knew I was in what had once been a bedroom. Whilst the décor in the office downstairs had been promiscuously abused by all and sundry, here the original wallpaper was still extant. One wall had obviously been composed of built-in wardrobes. These remained, but their doors had been removed. The wardrobes themselves had been fitted with shelves and these shelves were groaning under the weight of paper stacked on them. The doors themselves had been repurposed. Each was supported by two stacks of beer crates and served the current occupants as desks. A full length mirror was still fastened to one wall. It was obvious that this was a room occupied by people who were too busy keeping the organisation working to worry about trivia such as the office furniture.

By the time I arrived, the discussion had moved into the detail of our problem. As I entered, Laxey looked up and said, "Apparently the plans have been drawn for the house to be built in front of the shrine, and over the next week or so, they'll be delivering materials."

I asked, "So has Battass Droom in point of fact been confirmed in his role at our shrine?"

"No, that is to be confirmed at the next grand synod, which is in a month's time."

Laxey stood up. "Anyway we'd better be going."

One of the others stood up. "Where's your incumbent at the moment, it's just we've got this message for her but it's addressed to some flyspeck village in the mountains."

Laxey reached out and took the letter he was holding. He looked at the envelope. "Yes, it's for her, Aea alone knows why the address. I'll give it to her when we get back."

"Thanks. We did wonder."

We made our exit from the building. Once in Ropewalk and out of sight of the Office, I asked Laxey, "Well, are you going to open the envelope?"

"I'll leave that to Maljie, she'll be able to open and close it without leaving any traces."

We gathered in the Ostiary's cell that now housed the Deacon. It was felt that as a member of the diaconate he was technically the senior cleric currently present. At the very least this ensured that anything that happened would probably be regarded as 'his fault.' It has to be said I was impressed by the improvements he'd wrought. The curtain had been replaced by a door and the cell now boasted a sturdy table, a writing desk, and the bed was no longer just a paillasse on the floor. Still we had to bring our own chairs or perch on the edge of the bed. The room was rather crowded because Maljie had a guest, Madame Tiffy Weldonnan.

Now Madame Weldonnan was a great lady; a doyenne of society.

Yet for those who knew, there was a past. Tiffy Cust was a dancer, a chorus girl, before Mortimar Weldonnan laid siege to the stage door. Scandalously he married her and she bore him twelve children. The sons were burly, strong featured men taking after their father, and their daughters every bit as pretty and sharp as their mother. She had with her a young woman of barely seventeen, also called Tiffy, who was her youngest daughter. A pretty girl notable because of her long red hair and the expression of quiet amusement that never seemed far from her face. She was probably the image of her mother at that age. One difference was that she was accompanied by a rangy hound of uncertain temper. If I remember correctly her mother was more commonly remembered as dancing with a snake. The Weldonnan family had been friends of our shrine for a number of years, and Maljie and the older Tiffy had a long history of mutual acquaintance stretching back more years than a gentleman would attempt to recall. Laxey recounted our adventures and handed Maljie the letter. Maljie called for boiling water and then produced from somewhere about her person a knife with a long, slim, blade. She carefully opened the letter, setting the seal to one side for later. Then she read the letter aloud. Apparently it was from Battass Droom, expressing his sorrow at receiving our incumbent's resignation letter with regard to the Stairway Shrine and congratulating her in her appointment as archimandrite of a small shrine of devoted religious ladies so far north that it was apparently covered by snow for six months of the year.

It was perhaps unfortunate that Maljie was still holding the knife. With what I can only assume to be an expletive derived from the world of accounts and finance, she made a swift movement with her right hand and the knife was suddenly quivering in the door.

One of the mendicants muttered nervously, "So the falling in front of a runaway coach is back on the agenda?"

Quietly, Maljie said, "When we have finished with him, he'll look upon that as one of the perquisites of his position."

She turned to Laxey, "We have to delay the next Conclave of the Combined Hierarchs and their staffs. That's the only meeting that can formalise the situation. We also have to get the Incumbent in front of Conclave before they vote on her replacement."

From the cluster of mendicants sitting at the end of the table a small voice asked, "But what if she did resign?"

Before Maljie could answer one of the other mendicants slapped the first down with the comment, "Idiot, if she had resigned she'd have been a damned sight more cheerful when she left."

Maljie turned to me, "You will have to do something about this purported resignation letter. I'm sure Tiffy will help you get access."

Before either Tiffy or I could comment Laxey said, "How do we get the incumbent back, it could take six weeks or more. The next meeting of the Combined Hierarchs could be in three weeks."

"We'll send a messenger by balloon, if the wind is right it'll barely take two days to get there. Then with fast horses, it might be two weeks to get back. Given you're delaying the meeting, that shouldn't be a problem."

Our Deacon asked, "Who is the messenger?"

"Well I'm the only one who can fly the balloon." Then Maljie looked at me, "But I'll take Tallis with me, he's probably the lightest."

I felt the need to protest. "But I'm supposed to be doing something about the resignation letter."

"It'll take me at least a day to get the balloon ready. That should be plenty of time."

Chapter 4

As I left the meeting with both Tiffys and the large dog, I noticed Laxey in deep conversation with the Deacon. It was Madame Tiffy who came up with a plan for getting our hands on the resignation letter. She turned to Mistress Tiffy and said, "It's probably time you started earning a living."

Without turning a hair the younger woman said, "Of course Mamma. Have you any suggestions."

"I am sure some time working as a clerk for the Office of the Combined Hierophants of Aea would be a suitable post for a respectable young lady."

Her daughter nodded dutifully. "And of course I'd have a footman to ensure proper conduct."

Madam smiled at me, "I'm sure we have a jacket and britches in Tallis's size."

She ushered us to her coach, and once we were settled, she said, "My thought is I have a word with Cuddles."

"Cuddles?" I wasn't sure I knew the individual in question, at least not by that name.

"Yes, he's the Hierophant of the Temple of Aea in her Aspect as the Personification of Chastity. Cuddles and I go back a long way."

📖📖📖

It was the following evening when Madam's plan was executed. She had organised a dinner party, and, as wise hostess, asked me to be present. There were a dozen of us sitting round the table. At the head was Madam. She was seated between Mortimar, her husband, and the Hierophant.

To the left of the Hierophant was Shaleen, the chief virgin and temple dancer. Rather more importantly she was the Hierophant's mistress and had been for some decades.

I was seated next to Shaleen, and on my left was Connai. Now Connai was a legend, she must have been over eighty at the time of the meal, and yet she was slim, elegant, and had perfect poise and carriage. She was still a dancer and still taught dancing. She claimed to be feeling her age, as she could no longer put her foot behind her head.

On the other side of Mortimar was Maljie, and between her and Connai were two other couples of a similar age to the Weldonnans. One was Tagal Haswig and his wife Mellita. The other was Jos Bumblewin Junior with his wife Tiggi. As we sat and talked you would have been left guessing as to whether our company was a collection of former chorus girls and their husbands, or a group of successful usurers and their wives. Maljie (who had been both usurer and chorus girl, but not as far as I know, simultaneously) combined both trades in one person.

It was the Hierophant who sparked the conversation. With all the casualness of somebody dropping a large frog into a punch bowl he announced, "Hegumen Sydna is being suggested as our next Autocephalous Patriarch."

Given that everybody present had links with the Shine, this provoked interest.

Jos Bumblewin Junior asked, "Why, what's wrong with Telbat Spurt, our current Patriarch?

Maljie asked, "Apart from the obvious? Last week he drank too much at a dinner party I was present at. They were playing Keeps afterwards and I saw him stake his position and the entire property portfolio of the order on the turn of a card."

A little anxiously Tiggi asked, "But he did win?"

"Yes, briefly. Thanks to that card, the order was the biggest brothel keeper in Port Naain." Rather sadly she added, "Or we were until he managed to lose it again."

Shaleen said, "There's a feeling that it's time he retired from the burdens of active ministry so that he can give more time to contemplation."

Mortimar turned to Maljie. "Surely he has minders to ensure that he doesn't do anything too stupid."

"Yes, one was in the privy having a fit of the vapours when he saw what the Patriarch was doing. The other was playing erotic card games in one of the master bedrooms. They really need a better class of minders for him."

Connai asked, in tones of absolute innocence, "And what exactly were you doing, Maljie?"

"Somebody had to keep an eye on him so I joined in the game."

I asked, "So how did you do, it sounds like it was being played for dangerously high stakes?"

"It was only the turn of a card that stopped me becoming Autocephalous Patriarch."

After the dessert (a posset so thick, one had to eat it with a runcible spoon) I was asked to perform. I stood up and moved away from the table. Personally I dislike those who attempt to perform seated. Unless you are a recounter of anecdotes, you should always stand. I gave people time to shift their chairs slightly and started with a poem of mine, 'The Chorus Girl's Lament.' I'd written it for Tiffy some years ago and I knew it was a favourite of hers. Then I gave them a series of short mood pictures of Port Naain. This was something I had been working on and had vague plans of producing enough to be worth publishing as a separate work. Finally I gave them something no one had expected. Tagal Haswig slipped out and returned with Offan Valniggle, perhaps the finest guitarist in Port Naain.

Now forty years ago, an admirer had written some verses about Connai. These I'd found in a long forgotten collection of verse, and included with the stanzas, some simple notation so that it might be possible to sing them. I'd had a word with Tagal, who is one of Offan's patrons. Offan, once he had the notation and the words, and realising who they were for, had given the day to creating the music.

He arrived at the dinner table, bowed to the guests and played. Then he eventually nodded to me. At that point I started singing the words. Now I'm not a singer, but my voice is good enough not to embarrass a hostess. But blessedly Tiffy had thought to have the words copied and passed around her guests. The ladies, singers all, joined their voices with mine. The husbands did as wise men do, sat silent and adopted expressions of rapt attention.

The song came to an end and Offan brought the tune to a conclusion. Then he bowed and kissed Connai's hand, one master paying tribute to another. She smiled, wet-eyed, and kissed his cheek as he rose. Another chair was brought to the table and we shuffled along to allow Offan to sit next to Connai. From the kitchen a maid brought his dinner, kept warm for him. Nobody feeds Offan before a performance, he'll just ignore even the finest of foods, his mind caught up in chord sequences or whether he could try changing the fingering. As he ate and talked to Connai the rest of the table resumed their conversations. Maljie leaned forward a little to see past Mortimar, "How is young Tiffy proceeding with her choice of career?"

Madam shook her head sadly. "The girl won't take her nose out of a book, she wants to be a clerk of sorts." With that she leaned back and said to the maid who was siding away various dishes, "Please ask Mistress Tiffy to join us."

Two minutes later, Mistress Tiffy appeared. Now the red hair was tied up in a tight bun. Tiffy peered at the world through pince-nez and in her hands she clutched a book. I noted the title as she passed me to stand with her mother. It was 'The Greater Brevity, with Notes and Exposition.' More tedious books have doubtless been written, but it is a worthy challenger for the title. Most shrines will have a copy, and I suspected that that particular volume was ours. Rather dramatically, Madam turned to the Hierophant.

"Cuddles, my girl wants to explore her chosen career, ideally working for one of the temples. Is it possible you have a position vacant? Ideally somewhere menial that will put her off the idea for life."

The Hierophant shook his head. "I'm sorry Tiffy. In our temple, all our administration is done by people who are already ordained or who are on the path to ordination."

Next to him, Shaleen said thoughtfully, "Cuddles, what about the Office of the Combined Hierophants of Aea. Most of their people are drawn from the laity, and I'm sure there's someone there who owes you a favour."

Madam turned to him, "Could you Cuddles, I'd be so grateful."

Shaleen said, "Oh I'm sure he can arrange it."

From behind me, Connai said, dryly, "Girls, he's not an idiot. Don't treat him like one. If you want young Tiffy to work in that office for reasons of your own, just ask him."

The Hierophant stood and bowed to the older woman. "Thank you for that, Connai."

He sat down and looked at Madam Tiffy. "I will get her a job there, but I'd really like to know how much trouble I'm going to get into because of this."

Madam kissed him. "You'll get into no trouble whatsoever."

Suspiciously he asked, "So who will?"

Shaleen said, "Archhierophant Battass Droom."

The Hierophant smiled a gentle smile and turned to look at Mistress Tiffy. "You start tomorrow morning. Pray be punctual."

📖📖📖

There was the sound of knocking on the main door of the Shrine to Aea in her Aspect as the Personification of Tempered Enthusiasm. Our Deacon, realising he was the nearest person, living as he did in the ostiary's cell,

made his weary way to the door and opened it.
Facing him was a workman in a battered tunic.
"Where do you want this lot unloading?"
The Deacon peered past the workman and saw two
drays on the hard standing in front of the shrine. Both
were loaded with timber. Without hesitation he
gestured to the wall of the shrine. "Just stack it
there."
"What about the brick?"
"Brick?"
"Yeah, there's about a dozen drays of the bluidy stuff,
once we get them loaded."
At this point the Deacon realised things were starting
to get out of hand. He grabbed a gawping mendicant.
"Go and get Laxey. Now."

📖📖📖

Laxey looked at the chit the workman offered him.
Two drays loaded with timber. A dozen loaded with
brick. It was obvious that Battass Droom was wasting
no time when it came to building his new house.
Laxey pointed at the chit. "The idiots have got the
order wrong. The timber is for here, but the brick is
for the Shrine to Aea in her Aspect of Tendentious
Exegesis."
The workman just shook his head. "I does what the
chit tells me, mate."
Laxey smiled at him, took the chit, wrote on the new
directions. The workman studied the new chit. "But
it's in Avitas!"
"Yes. They're always getting us mixed up. Not only
are the names a bit similar, we're in Exegesis Square.
It confuses everybody. So just book your brick onto a
barge and send it there."
The workman looked worried. Laxey smiled at him
again. "Look we'll get the mendicants to unload the
first wagon then you can get back and tell your boss
to send the bricks by barge. Then we'll get the second
one unloaded whilst you're away."

As the second empty dray made its way across Exegesis Square Laxey turned to the Lector. "So what in the forty-seven hells are we going to do with all this wood?"

The Lector sounded a little defensive. "But it's all good stuff, it'll always come in for something."

Laxey gestured at the pile, "There's a fair heap of it."

"Yes, but I might have an idea. I'll just see if the offer of a ship's mast is still open."

⚏⚏⚏

Dressed as a footman I handed Mistress Tiffy into her mother's coach, stepped aside to allow her great hound to jump effortlessly in and then went to stand on the position at the back of the coach. The coachman grinned at me and cracked his whip. We were in motion. I confess that I was not in an entirely good humour. I had risen early, walked an hour across town, and had arrived at Madam Tiffy's establishment soaked to the skin in the early morning rain. I had been presented with a large towel, and the outfit of a footman. The jacket was a little long but at least it hid the fact that the britches were too large and were held up by a belt and braces.

We then drove back much of the way I had walked, with me catching the tail end of the rain. Not only that but the Periwig, whilst stable enough on its own, was distinctly prone to wobble thanks to the large formal bicorn that I had to wear as part of the outfit. Knowing Madam Tiffy's past, I assume my current uniform was acquired from a theatrical outfitter rather than one of those discreet emporia which provide the uniforms for the servant classes.

Still it has to be admitted that travelling at the back of a coach does have its advantages. You see so much more. Indeed at one point we passed a ship's mast being carried on the shoulders of a score of mendicants.

That isn't something you often see. Also, thanks to the wig and the ridiculously large hat, I was probably unrecognisable, so I was unlikely to face ridicule from my peers.

When we arrived at the Office of the Combined Hierophants the coach drew smoothly to a halt and I somewhat stiffly leapt down, lowered the step and handed Mistress Tiffy out of the coach. The dog followed, jumping down with far more lithe grace than I had managed and proceeded to intimidate the doorman by grinning at him. Mistress Tiffy led the way into the building, with me, a symphony in pink, following, carrying a picnic basket. The doorman, keeping cautiously to his cubbyhole enquired about our business.

Tiffy produced a slip of paper which she read but didn't offer to show him. "I am here to take up an offer of employment in the personnel section."

Still with one eye on the dog, the doorman leaned out of the cubbyhole and pointed down a corridor. "It's the door at the end. There's nobody in, what with there being no one working there until you came. But I'll ring for Brassnet and he'll come and put you right."

We made our way down the corridor and I slipped ahead to open the door to allow Mistress Tiffy to enter. Even as we stood looking round at a very large room stuffed full with free standing shelving, there was a low growl from the dog. It wasn't loud, just pitched perfectly so that you felt the hairs on the back of your legs stand up. I turned to see an elderly and somewhat harassed clerk enter. "Good morning, I am Brassnet, you must be Tiffy Weldonnan?"

"Yes, I am the younger Tiffy Weldonnan. I have come to take up a position here, in personnel."

Brassnet gestured around. "It's quite simple
. In this room, on the various shelves, we have a pigeon hole for every ordained person in the order. On the back wall we have a somewhat larger receptacle for every shrine.

Each of these receptacles has the names of all those formally connected with the shrine or institution. Documents relating to ordained persons go into their pigeon hole. Documents pertaining to the lesser lights go into the receptacle that is linked to their shrine. Your job is to firstly file any documents you are given in the right place. Then if asked for documents pertaining to a person or institution you should retrieve them from the correct place. Also occasionally you will receive information to update the personnel at a particular shrine or institution."

He smiled, a little shyly. "It's actually perfectly simple, but if you do have problems, just stick your head out of the door and shout, 'Brassnet'. It's what everybody else does."

With that he backed out of the room and disappeared. I put the picnic basket down on the desk. On the desk was a wicker tray filled with documents. Tiffy glanced at a couple. "These seem to be for filing."

"First things first, we have to find the incumbent's file."

I went to the nearest shelf. "It seems to be arranged by the date of ordination."

"That's useful," Tiffy commented, "When was she ordained."

"I don't have the faintest idea, I'm not even sure how old she is."

"Just count her teeth, works every time."

I glanced at the young woman, I had suspected she had a dry sense of humour but it's always as well to check these things, a chap can get into a lot of trouble just making assumptions.

Eventually, after a lot of searching, we found the right pigeonhole. I emptied it and flicked through the heap of documents it produced. There were two that immediately interested me.

The first was the purported resignation, the second was the appointment to the position of archimandrite of a small shrine of Far Upper Icegill.

(There are apparently three shrines, the larger main convent is Lower Icegill, the secondary one is Upper Icegill, and the tertiary one is Far Upper Icegill. I've know the incumbent suggest that Maljie might like to spend some time there exploring her vocation, normally when things have got entirely out of hand.)

Tiffy examined them. "What do we do with them?"

"Well the letter of resignation we have to replace with a more obvious forgery. As for the letter of appointment I'm not sure. We could just misfile it. After all, our incumbent's pigeonhole has at least one document relating to Farrat Than, the incumbent at the Shrine to Aea in her Aspect of Tendentious Exegesis. Given that they weren't even ordained in the same decade, I suspect somebody thought they'd got the right shrine and just dumped it there to be rid of it. Alternately we could change the name and give some other person the job. Or just destroy the damned thing altogether."

"Who should we send there?"

"Honestly I'm not sure there is any lady I dislike enough to inflict that place on her. Indeed those who most need it aren't ordained so aren't eligible."

"Perhaps you should just take it back to the shrine and let people discuss it?"

"And let Maljie decide who deserves to go?" Tiffy looked pensive, so I added, "Maljie's list of people who appear to have avoided the rightful vengeance of the 'Kindly Ones' is a long one."

I looked closely at the letter of appointment. "Look, I can just add a couple of strokes to a letter or two in the name of the person appointed. It's unlikely that there is anybody of that name. Then we can misfile it. So even if it's found, it'll just be misfiled again as too much trouble to deal with."

Tiffy nodded, still a little pensive. "Is this how bureaucracies work?"

"Only the good ones. May Aea spare us the torment of living under an efficient bureaucracy."

I made the appropriate pen strokes and took the altered appointment letter to the far side of the stacks and added it to the pigeonhole of a middle aged ordained monk of untroubled sanctity. When I arrived back, Tiffy was examining the letter of resignation. She looked up, a worried look on her face. "What if it's real?"

"It isn't, Maljie said so."

"Maljie hasn't seen the letter, she might be wrong."

I glanced round dramatically, "Aea be my witness that I never said then."

I winked at her. "Let me have a look at the letter."

I read it carefully. "Look here. Every time our shrine is mentioned, the writer gives it the full name, the Shrine to Aea in her Aspect as the Personification of Tempered Enthusiasm. Whenever she writes, our incumbent gives us full title the first time, and then just calls us the Stairway Shrine from then on."

I looked further, "And here, below her signature, where she's printed her name. She's spelled her first name wrong. It's not a bad forgery but it is a forgery."

"So what do we do with it?"

"You copy it out. Try to copy the handwriting." I looked round. "Ah yes, here's some of the headed paper from Office of the Combined Hierophants. Cut off the heading and write on that. I'll do the signature."

"It won't be very good."

"Good enough to pass muster provided nobody produces a specimen of the incumbent's hand writing."

There was a growl from the dog, followed by a knock on the door. I opened it and Brassnet stood there.

"Excuse me but this 'individual' wishes to speak to Tallis Steelyard."

Looking down at the very junior mendicant standing next to him I could see why he had been hesitant about assigning a gender.

It was only a week since Maljie had all the
mendicants shaved as a precaution against lice. Not
only that, but the child was wearing a hooded robe
that would render even the most full-bosomed
androgynous.

The child looked up at me. On limited evidence I
would have assumed it was female.

"Maljie asks, 'are you going to take all day?' The
balloon is ready and she wants to set off while the
wind is right."

I picked up a pen, scrawled a reasonable copy of the
incumbent's signature, but with the wrong spelling.

"Tiffy, I'm afraid I'll have to abandon you."

"But we fetched a picnic lunch for two."

I gestured to the mendicant. "She'll help you, both
with filing and eating."

With that I made my exit. Even as I jogged through
the building, (winning myself the glares of clerks,
shocked at anything moving at more than a glacial
crawl) I was trying to work out my best route.
Regretfully I decided that the detour back to the
barge to change my clothes was probably a step too
far. Once in the street I headed by the shortest route
to the Stairway Shrine.

There on the cleared area was an inflated balloon,
tugging on the ropes that were holding it down.

Picking my way through piles of lumber, I arrived at
the balloon.

Maljie glared at me, "I thought I'd have to leave
without you."

"You might have to, unless I can get something else
to wear."

"We're going to a monastery, nobody will care what
you wear."

"I assume it's going to be cold up there. This suit
verges on the flimsy."

Maljie turned to a nearby mendicant, "You, take off
your robe and give it to Tallis."

"Me?" The voice was definitely female.

"Probably best not," Maljie turned and cast an eye over the other mendicants. "You're a big one, we'll have your robe."

"I'll need shoes as well."

"You're wearing shoes."

"I can feel the cobbles through the holes in the soles." The mendicant, now standing in his small clothes, handed me a robe. He looked sadly down at the heavy sandals he was wearing. "But I only just got a pair that fitted."

"And his are too big anyway," I added.

"It's all fuss, fuss, fuss." Maljie surveyed the throng who were watching the performance with interest. "Who here has smallish feet?"

"Clean smallish feet," I added.

A pair of sandals was passed through the crowd to me. I tried them on, they fitted.

Maljie beckoned me to join her in the balloon. "Well is there anything else you want, a parasol perhaps, or a hat in a different style?"

I climbed in to the basket. Even as I did, the ropes were cast off and we were airborne. A better hat would have been nice though.

Chapter 5

Now at this point, I as the narrator face a quandary. Do I continue with my tale or should I change tack and devote this chapter to the antics of Laxey and Tiffy? As is my wont when perplexed, I discussed this matter with Shena, my lady wife. She pointed out that the reader knows I survive, in spite of the dangers, hardships and privations that I might face. After all, I'm the one telling the story. But the fate of Laxey, Tiffy, and even more the fate of her great dog, hang in the balance. The reader might well wish to be reassured about their fates.

This seems a not unreasonable attitude to adopt and yet I feel that art demands a little more doubt and uncertainty. So driven by my muse I have decided to continue with my adventures. Some have suggested that I wrote them in epic verse. But I demurred.

Epic verse
If terse
Is worse
Than prose
To reassure
Or obscure
The poor
Reader

Thus, as I grasped the rim of the basket, I watched the ground recede at considerable speed. Even as the people below grew smaller I was aware that we were also moving at a reasonable pace to the north-east. Maljie glanced at her compass. "I think a little higher, the wind is stronger up there. I want to get as far as I can before dark."
"What do we do when it's dark?"
"Keep going and hope we're high enough to miss the ground."
I confess that I have always loved travelling by balloon. I have not done it often, but the silence and the view are to be cherished. I suppose I was bad company, thinking my own thoughts, drinking up the scenery, and occasionally jotting down a few notes, bits of verse that caught in my imagination.

One can travel forever
At a height that gives you a perspective
That mocks human endeavour
And encourages the introspective
To cherish the zephyr
That lifts them above the merely reflective.

Ah but a balloon flight is a terrible thing for a poet, however much he enjoys it.

Still, as evening was falling, Maljie opened the picnic basket and we dined on a large pasty, the meat succulent and the gravy rich and clotted around the vegetables. A couple of glasses of white wine, followed by fruit, completed our repast. Maljie then topped up the reservoir on the burner with pure spirit and we sat and talked quietly, watching the mountains draw nearer. Already we were at considerable height and the air was cold. I pulled my mendicant's robe close. Indeed I was glad of the periwig as it helped keep my head warm. I pondered the bicorn, wondering if I could somehow unfold it so it would protect my ears but the material was far too rigid.

It was as we chatted and I fiddled with the hat I asked Maljie a question I had pondered for some time. "How did you end up serving Aea? You were a successful usurer."

She leaned back against the basket and passed me a bottle of beer. "The answer is simple, or else remarkably complicated, Aea asked me to."

I waited for her to elucidate and as I looked up from the hat I realised she was looking at me quizzically. "I felt a hand on my shoulder in an empty room. I nearly wet myself. When I was back in control of myself, I looked round to see somebody standing there. They seemed to glow from within. The 'somebody' smiled at me and said, "I need you." They then just disappeared. I already had an invitation to dine later that day with a friend who was attached to one of the shrines. When I arrived at her house, she took one look at me and said, "Aea spoke to you didn't she?"

Maljie shrugged. "When you've had a personal invitation it seems rude not to accept it. So I abandoned usury and changed direction. I did all sorts of things, looking after those in the Insane Asylum, at one point I was feeding orphans.

I kept thinking I was on top of a project and could perhaps ease up a bit, and suddenly a new project would come along. Finally I got dumped here at the shrine. It's not a bad place to wash up when you're not perhaps as young as you once were."

I sat in silence. There isn't a lot you can say. Then I asked, "And now we're on a madcap quest to find our incumbent."

By the light of the burner I could see Maljie's face clearly. She smiled. "Yes. We're helping to stamp on some petty, mindless self-aggrandisement that needs squashing. Otherwise if it isn't checked it spreads and corrupts everything it touches. You'll find that you can become very unpopular very quickly when you do kick back against it. But it's a good sort of unpopularity. It's an unpopularity to cherish, because you can judge how well you're doing by just who dislikes you."

She fell silent, leaning against the basket. Then meditatively she said, "When you come across this sort of corruption spreading through an organisation that you love because of the good it can do, even if it does so much of it by accident, you have to tear it out by the roots and burn it."

"Why didn't you get ordained?"

She sighed. "Look round any temple or shrine, Tallis. You'll see a lot of decent people, nice people, people who it's easy to like. Out there, beyond the walls of the shrine, are a lot of bad people who know what they ought to do. They might even want to do the right thing. But they're afraid because to them doing the right thing can be a slippery slope and they fear where it may take them. So somebody has to hold their hand, keep them from the gallows, give them reasons they can accept for doing what they know they ought to do. I hold their hand and make sure they don't do a pratfall and break their necks on the slippery slope. I don't need to be ordained to do that."

I watched as she got to her feet to check the burner. Still thinking of her words I dozed off.

⊞⊞⊞

Watching the dawn over the mountains can be
spectacular. But it is even more spectacular if you
watch it from a balloon flying at a ridiculous height.
The air seemed thin as well as deathly cold. We were
now 'in' the mountains, the foothills were behind us. I
noticed Maljie seemed a little concerned. Wary of
saying anything I waited as she studied the compass
and tapped the burner to ensure it was burning
freely.

"It's going to be close."

I looked ahead. There was a pass in front of us,
indeed we were already higher than it. "What is the
problem?"

"I think we'll miss the pass. We're going too far to the
north."

I looked again. If you sighted along the compass you
could see that we would miss the main body of the
col. Still the north side didn't rise as steeply as the
south, indeed it was almost stepped. So it was
entirely possible we would ground on what I already
thought of as the first step.

"Can we go higher?"

"Not a lot."

We both watched. As we drew closer it was obvious
that we were going to come to rest on the first step
at the point where it pushed steadily upwards
towards the north.

I started lashing the picnic hamper to a rope. It was
obvious that we had to lose weight, and probably
quite a lot weight. "Right, as we get closer, I'll go
down the rope with the basket, drop the rope after
me when I've landed and hopefully you'll get over and
I'll walk back."

It probably wasn't the wisest suggestion I've ever
made but Maljie nodded and helped me lift the basket
over the side. Below I could see our shadow rushing
across the snowfield, catching up with us.

As it grew closer, Maljie said, "Now."

I lowered the basket and then climbed down the rope after it. The basket hit the ground with a bump and I dropped the last few feet into a snow bank. The rope fell around me. I pulled myself out of the snow and watched as the balloon cleared the crest of the ridge but only just. Then as it disappeared from view I got to my feet, coiled the rope and retrieved the picnic hamper.

I carried the basket to where the wind had blown the snow off the rocks. I sat on the basket and cut my hat in two. Now I had two wedge shaped pieces. I slid my sandaled feet into them and then used the thongs fastening the hamper to fasten the improvised overshoes to my feet. I then looked in the hamper, deciding that it was easier to eat a good breakfast than it was to carry the food on my back. I ate bread and cheese and washed it down with the rest of the wine. I then filled the bottle with water from a rill that trickled out from under the snow. I used the rope to make a sling so I could carry the hamper, which contained two bottles of beer and enough bread and cheese for a meal, and started to descend.

Now, it spite of comments made about my faculties by other, lesser, poets, I am not totally witless. Even as I hoisted the hamper over the side of the balloon's basket, I was studying the terrain. The col dropped down but not too steeply and there were places clear of snow, so it should be possible to walk down without having to wade up to my waist through snow drifts. Also, a long way below, I had seen smoke, such as might rise from a chimney. So I had a possible destination. I made my way towards the rock. The sun was now playing across the surface and the thin ice that had formed overnight was thawing. Also I could see the narrow paths left by wild orid or beillie. With it being summer they probably came this far up to graze on the various mosses and sparse herbage.

I suppose that had I been Urlan I would have abandoned everything to go off and hunt them, and would have eventually arrived at my destination with a fine carcass draped across my shoulders. Given I am a poet, I beg leave to doubt whether I would have much success bringing down such an elusive prey, armed as I was with a picnic hamper. Still the thought amused me as I picked my way carefully down the slope. Soon I was able to follow the paths for some distance, taking advantage of them when they ran in the direction I was heading and abandoning them and going my own way they didn't. The scenery was magnificent. Every so often I would stop to gaze across the stunning vista. In all candour I always feel a little unworthy at times like this. Yes I enjoyed the view. I was overwhelmed with the beauty, had I had company, I would have fallen silent. Yet I always feel that as a poet under these circumstances I should think sublime thoughts and produce deathless verse. As it was, my thoughts tended to major on the fact that my sandals were starting to pinch and my stomach was rumbling.

It made for a long, weary, day. Tramping uphill is hard, but downhill is no easier. It puts far more strain on your knees and I felt the lack of a sturdy staff as several times the dirt would move under my descending foot and I was in danger of tumbling. Given the steepness of the slope, a tumble would go on for a long time. At some points, it might even last the rest of my life.

Still the day was not unpleasant. The sun remained out and I even started to feel warm enough to allow my robe to hang loose around me. I stopped once to rest and to eat a little and sip some more of my water. Whilst I rested I tried to plan the next stage of my journey. Ahead of me a spur jutted out and from memory I needed to take the left or southern side of it if I wished to reach the source of the smoke I'd seen earlier.

I picked up my burden and set off once again. Now I was low enough for the ground to be covered with a fine crop of heather. Fortunately there were more paths and the slope was less steep. I was making better time. As I got down to the level of the spur I could see that there was a path which ran along the crest and then curved and made its way down the south side. I made my way to join it. Once I was walking it I could tell that it had been made by man. In certain particularly steep sections, stones had been firmly dug in so that they acted like a flight of stairs. Eventually, as evening was falling, the path led me to the edge of a small dell. Here, nestling amongst the first grass that I had seen, was a small stone hut. Sitting outside, obviously watching my arrival with interest, was a man who was dressed in a similar robe to the one I wore. I had obviously fallen in with a hermit of some sort.

He stood up, a little stiffly, as I approached. He was obviously old, his hood had fallen down over his shoulders and what little was left of his hair was white. Even his bushy eyebrows were greying. As he pulled himself up to his full height I could see he was tall. In his youth he must have been a big, powerful man. Now he was gaunt and stooped but still stood a head taller than me.

"This morning I was out and about. I go up to the end of the spur, sit there and meditate. Out of the west came a balloon which just crested the ridge. Some hours later I see before me a mendicant who has reached late middle age without entering the order, and still wears pink. I suspect there is a story here worth telling."

I bowed. "I am Tallis Steelyard. I was forced to abandon the balloon so that my companion could gain height and press on with our quest."

He leaned back and stared up towards the pass. "A companion, you say. Does this companion have a name, and what in the name of Aea was your quest?"

"My companion was Maljie, senior temple warden from the Shrine to Aea in her Aspect as the Personification of Tempered Enthusiasm in Port Naain."

He smiled, broadly. "When I saw the balloon, Maljie did come to mind. I can see that you do indeed have a story worth telling." He gestured at the setting sun. "The day is fading. You will need something to eat and somewhere to sleep tonight. Come on in."

☐☐☐

The stone hut was low but snug. Even I couldn't stand upright except in the middle under the ridge pole. Along one wall was a box bed, the sides were pieces of flat stone, the mattress was dried heather. There was a flat topped stone that my companion used as a table, he sat cross legged on the floor. We dined on a meal made from our combined resources, cheese, bread, onions, some bean pottage flavoured with wild herbs, and a bottle of beer each. As we ate he told me a little of himself. His name was Gord Roseban. He had found this hut many years ago and in later life had refurbished it and had come up here to spend his final years in quiet meditation. He had a small vegetable patch and every couple of weeks somebody came up from one of the farms further down the hill, bringing him supplies.

At one point, greatly daring, I asked whether he knew Maljie.

He nodded. "Yes, a lot of years ago I knew her. I was working in Avitas at the time. I felt called to build a refuge, somewhere for the young, the old, the destitute or those who have just been broken by life. I came to Port Naain because it occurred to me that in that city I could perhaps find the funds I needed. After all there are many wealthy shrines, surely in one of them the love of Aea could still be found. Instead I was advised to seek funds from wealthy donors.

I was at one social event and somebody pointed out a young woman talking to a couple of older men. My informant prodded me and said, "That's Maljie, she's been touched by Aea. She's destined for great things."

I felt I had to be polite so I merely asked, "She is?"

"Oh yes, she's been asked to raise money, then she is to go as an advisor to our new priest in Tideholt."

"Tideholt?" I confess I'd never heard the name.

"A pretty town far to the east, it lies on the Southern Ocean. A pleasant climate, wide sandy beaches, excellent local wines. Apparently there was once a shrine to Aea there and it has been decided to send a team to rebuild and re-sanctify it. Apparently Maljie is in for two years of exotic travel and fine living."

I bowed to my companion and walked across to Maljie. She obviously noticed me walking across to her because she said something to her two companions, stepped away from them and waited for me to speak.

"Maljie, I believe you are heading away for two years."

"Word travels doesn't it? Yes, I'm off to Tideholt and apparently I'll be away for two years if not more."

"Maljie, I'd like you to give me those two years, I'm creating a refuge in Avitas."

Old Gord fell silent, lost in thought, then he said to me, "We talked for an hour or more that evening. Next day she gave backword to those organising the Tideholt trip. She raised money for me in Port Naain, she came with me to Avitas where she not merely raised more money, she bullied builders into doing their job properly. She cajoled local dignitaries to waive rules and regulations over who could build what, and where. She faced down local crime lords who wanted a cut of our money, and she joined the dunnykindivers in cleaning out the dunnypits. In two years she had helped me create my refuge, then she was called to another project and we lost touch."

He put down his empty beer bottle. "So what is your story?"

I had already decided it was going to be far easier to just tell him the whole truth. Told properly the tale took until dark. He recognised some of the names, but others had appeared on the scene long after his day. Battass Droom he vaguely remembered, a minor clerk in holy orders. Shaleen he remembered as well. He remembered her as a young woman and was willing to swear nobody before or since could match her as a dancer. Eventually he banked up the small fire, for it gets cold at night so high in the mountains, and he slept on his mattress and I curled up on the floor, wrapped in my robe. Sleep came easily that night.

Chapter 6

Tiffy looked at the small figure in the mendicant's robe. "Right, can you read?"

"An' write." The incumbent insisted. "An' Maljie teaches them as don't want to learn."

"Good. Can you take this basket and put the papers in the right pigeon hole. It'll take a while for us to work out where everybody is. While you do that I'll write this letter."

The mendicant reached for the basket. "Yes miss."

"I'm called Tilley. What are you called?"

"Well me Da said to call me 'Snotty' until I decided on my own name."

Tiffy was horrified. "Your father said that?"

"Well he ain't me Da really, he's me sponsor. I'm almost an orphan."

Tiffy was familiar with the concept. The order would accept orphans but rather liked a sponsor to stay in touch with them so that they didn't lose touch with the outside world. "Who are your sponsors?"

"Mad Jez an' 'is woman, Athica."

Tiffy could understand why the girl child in front of

her carried herself with such self-confidence. Mad Jez wasn't as young as he had been, but he was still the most dangerous freelance thug in the city. The child continued. "Jez is a big softy, he give us a kitten and he'll sit wi' us an' play with it."

With this she picked up the basket and disappeared in between the racks of shelves. Tiffy pondered the complexities of human nature and then got on with writing the letter over the signature Tallis had put at the bottom of the sheet of paper.

Finished, she looked at her work. The handwriting was similar, which was probably all that was needed. On careful examination she realised she'd spelled 'hermeneutics' and 'exegesis' incorrectly, but that was probably all to the good as well. Anyway, they struck her as remarkably silly words in include in a resignation letter. She sanded the letter, addressed it, folded it and took it to the appropriate pigeon hole.

Snotty appeared at her side. "I'm done."

"Any problems?"

"No, once you know where people are and can hold the pattern in your head, it's easy."

Tiffy looked on her young companion with new eyes. "Snotty, I think this is a job you can do."

Snotty gave a sad smile. "They'll never give a job like this ter the likes of me."

Tiffy could see the truth in her comment. "Right, so we'll have to do something about this. We'll change the name for a start. Have you got a name you want to be called?"

"Not really."

"Then for now we'll call you 'Eudicea'. I have an aunt called that, she's my father's sister and she was horrified when he married Mother and hasn't spoken to him since."

"Eudicea." She tried the name to see if it fitted. "Yeah, I like that."

There was a knock at the door.

Tiffy shouted, "Come in."

Brassnet stuck his head round the door. "It's time for lunch. Some time ago, in an effort to be collegial, I suggested that those of us working on the ground floor dined together in the old kitchen. Everybody fetches their own lunch but I boil a kettle and we share a pot of infusion."

Tiffy smiled warmly at him. "How delightful. The three of us will be along immediately."

Grabbing the picnic basket she led Eudicea and the hound into the kitchen. It was quite a large room which appeared to be little used save for storage. Brassnet had obviously managed to keep an area clear around the stove. This he had lit and was keeping burning by feeding it with office detritus. There was a small table at which were seated two young men. Brassnet introduced them as Glenan and Filby. Tiffy helped Eudicea into one of the remaining seats and then sat down herself. "I am Tiffy, this is Eudicea and the dog is Spot."

The two young men glanced in awed fascination as the rangy, all-black, hound took its place next to the stove."

"Spot," Filby said, tentatively."

"I was young when I named him."

Brassnet took the remaining seat and opened a small packet of sandwiches wrapped in waxed paper. This was obviously the sign for everybody to start on their own meal.

Brassnet asked, "So how is the planning going for the next meeting of Combined Hierophants?"

Glenan stopped dunking his bread in his mug of infusion. "We'll probably have the room ready, but it'll be touch and go."

Filby nodded his agreement. "It was a good idea but they should have started work six months earlier."

Brassnet gestured to Tiffy and Eudicea. "Remember these two ladies don't know what you're talking about."

Glenan rose in his seat, bowed, and sat down again.

"Sorry, yes. Basically when the Combined Hierophants meet we need a large room for them, their advisors and senior hangers-on. Up until now they would meet in one of the larger temples. They'd take turns, each acting as host. The problem was that each felt they were at a disadvantage when it wasn't their temple. So there was all sorts of politicking to ensure you had the right meeting with the right agenda in the right temple."

Filby took up the tale. "So somebody came up with the idea of converting the upper attics here into one room which would be big enough for the meeting."

Tiffy asked, "But isn't there a house in the way?"

Glenan said, "Strangely enough, that isn't a problem. The old woman's husband sold their attic to the order many years ago to make sure that his widow didn't have to worry about the roof. So we had no problems from that direction."

"On the other hand," Filby said, "We've discovered a lot of timbers were in a pretty poor state and even the good ones needed raising to ensure we got the right amount of head room."

"But will you be finished in time?" Brassnet asked.

"It'll be close but we should do it." Glenan glanced at Filby as he spoke. The other young man said, "Just don't look too closely at the decoration."

Tiffy asked, "Why, what will be wrong with it?"

Glenan sighed. "Let's just say it will be the perfect opportunity for the artist who wants to produce a true fresco. Unfortunately he'll have to work when the Hierophants are meeting because by my reckoning, that's when the plaster will be going on."

"Can you hurry things?" Tiffy asked. She remembered Maljie's comment about making sure the meeting was delayed.

"We're trying, but we don't want to cut corners, or have to go back and redo various pieces of work."

"Is it possible for me to see what's going on?" Tiffy asked.

Filby stood and bowed. "Madam, it would be my pleasure to show you around when you've eaten."

📖📖📖

Tiffy led Laxey and the Deacon to one of the upper windows in the Stairway Shrine. As they made their way through the building she had described the conversation over lunch. As they finally looked out of a window, Tiffy studied the streetscape ahead of her. "I could see this window of the shrine from the attic room, so I should be able to see the attic room from here. Especially as whilst I kept Filby talking, Eudicea managed to hang out of the window the red cloth our lunch was wrapped in."

Laxey pointed. "I can see it."

Tiffy looked where he was pointing. "Yes that's it. The big meeting room is just under the roof. In fact they've stripped out the attic ceilings, panelled off some of the roof and put in a higher ceiling right down the middle. I just wondered if you could have somebody pull a lot of tiles off if it rains, then it'll do a lot of damage and we can blame the weather."

Laxey said, "It's an option. Is there any other way of slowing them down to get a cancellation?"

"I'll keep my ears open." Tiffy stopped and stared at the Deacon who had taken out a compass and was taking a bearing on the red cloth. He looked up to see both Laxey and Tiffy now watching him with interest. "Don't mind me, I've just had an idea."

With that he jotted down the bearing and disappeared down the stairs.

Laxey stared into the distance. "Are you going to keep working there?"

"Yes, I've discovered Eudicea is a natural for the job, so I'll stay and can keep an eye on things whilst she does the job."

"That's good," Laxey said absently, it was obvious that he was running various ideas through his mind and he wasn't really listening.

Tiffy continued. "So it's sensible that she might as well come and live with us so we can have her dressed properly. There's no shortage of clothes, we've still got drawers of 'hand-me-downs.'" Laxey merely nodded absently so Tiffy continued, "Which means her brother will have to live with us as well. It's not as if we're short of rooms, what with so many of us having grown up and left home." She waiting a minute or two. Laxey was totting things up on his fingers. So Tiffy said, "I'm glad you're agreeable to this. I must go and organise things."

Laxey suddenly focussed on the conversation. "Pardon?"

He was speaking to himself, Tiffy had already left.

📖📖📖

Laxey made his way slowly downstairs. As far as he could see, there were three ways of delaying the meeting. One was delaying the work on the building, a second was somehow making sure that the Hierophants of Aea couldn't be there. The third method would be to have the administration reschedule it. He rather dismissed the first method. Climbing on roofs and pulling slates off, or even breaking in and doing damage, could so easily go wrong. Indeed when you go out of your way to cross powerful and vindictive people, you really have to have your alibi in place long before you need it. Also it ought to be a really solid alibi. People would start looking for culprits. Indeed he suspected that for Battass Droom, their shrine would be an obvious place to start the search for people to blame. Persuading the administration to reschedule had potential. The problem here was that whilst it could be done, whoever did it would have to have both an excellent reason and the hide of a brontothere to shrug off the fury of all those whose diaries had suddenly been dislocated.

Laxey had run a quick tally of who he knew who might be able to organise it, but felt he was short of favours to call in.

This left him with the option of making sure the Hierophants couldn't be at the meeting. It was then he realised how little notice he'd taken of the Hierophants previously. He knew the temples they were formally attached to but his knowledge stopped at that. Then he remembered Philiman, the theologically sanctioned beggar.

To break into the thread of the narrative here, it's worth explaining about Philiman and his role. One issue faced by senior hierophants is that they are expected to be charitable. Between ourselves I have no problems with that. But there again, if they are seen to give money to beggars who spend it on drink or sensual indulgence, then the hierophants will find their actions attacked. Often by smug and prosperous people who also spent their money on drink and sensual indulgence. So it's vitally important to have the 'right sort of beggars' there to be given alms.

The temple bureaucracy considered the matter and decided that rather than have to scrutinise a new selection of beggars for every event, it was sensible merely to have one worthy recipient of the hierophants' charity, and that person would be included as part of the proceedings. The role of the theologically sanctioned beggar was born. Philiman was selected as the first incumbent of the position. It has to be admitted that he fitted the criteria perfectly. He was not merely ascetic in his habits, his only indulgence was soap and water. Thus he was clean. Also what monies he received that he didn't need to support his own meagre lifestyle, he cheerfully shared with other worthy recipients.

But from Laxey's point of view, the important point wasn't Philiman's way of life, it was the fact that he had to be present whenever a hierophant made a formal public appearance. Indeed hierophants might even summon him to receive alms on their informal appearances, if they felt that there might be an adequate supply of bystanders to witness the gesture. So Philiman was the perfect person to discuss the whereabouts and activities of the hierophants. He was issued with their timetable up to six months ahead. Laxey made his way to the Temple of Aea in Her Aspect of the Personification of Chastity. Philiman had a 'room' there. In reality it was a hut the size of a dog kennel, built onto the outside wall. There he would sit when not formally working, soliciting alms from passers-by and reading theological tracts of magnificent opacity.

When he arrived at the kennel, Laxey dropped a twenty dreg into the brass bowl.

Philiman looked up, "Still trying to pass off forged coins, Laxey. That one has more lead in it that a respectable coin should have."

Laxey squatted down beside him. "Just trying to attract your attention. I need to tap your wisdom."

"In that case, a lead twenty is probably overpayment. What can I help you with?"

"It's quite simple. Some of our mendicants have been asking about the next meeting of the Combined Hierophants."

"Ah, the formal conclave."

"That's the one. What exactly happens and can our mendicants go and watch any of it?"

Philiman squirmed, scratching his back on the edge of his kennel. "Better than that, they can take part."

Laxey was a little surprised at that. "They can?"

"Yes, remember the Conclave is the last stage in the proceedings. Four days before the Conclave, the Hierophants gather together at the Shrine of Aea Reimagined, South of the River. There they will hold a silent retreat and fast from sunrise to sunset. The evening meals are simple affairs, often just a salad with a few beans.

The breakfasts tend to be hearty, consisting of as much thick unsweetened porridge as you want.

On the final day there is a formal meal, at which they can talk and eat. This meal does tend towards the lavish.

On the following day they walk in solemn procession from the shrine to the ferry, then from the ferry to the place of meeting. If your mendicants are reasonably scrubbed up there's no reason why they shouldn't join the procession. Certainly when they cross the ferry they're often met by contingents from quite a few of the shrines."

Laxey meditated on this. "And at the Shrine of Aea Reimagined, could there be a role for our mendicants there?"

"Sometimes you do get parties who gather to pray for the success of the Conclave. That used to be more popular than it is now. I've seen scores of people gathered to share the fast and silent retreat."

Laxey stood up. "Thank you for that. You've given me something to think about. I can give the mendicants some options to consider."

Chapter 7

Even as she dropped the rope down to Tallis, Maljie felt the balloon rise. It was still rising as it crested the ridge, causing a family of lichen gatherers to panic. Her balloon sailed onwards and she was looking down into a long deep valley which ran north to south below her. Mentally she compared the terrain below her to the chart she had brought with her. The map was a composite. She had sketched the lands west of the pass she had just crossed from her own experience. She'd never previously crossed the pass but had seen it in the far distance on another trip. The terrain to the east of the pass she'd taken from a sketch map that she'd found in a book, 'The Apophthegmata of the Hesychasts and Cenobites.' It dwelt especially on those who lived in the mountains and attempted mark the approximate location of hermitages and monasteries.

The problem was that she wasn't sure if this valley was the right one, or whether there was another pass that she had to cross. Her balloon continued to rise as she burned more spirit. She scanned the mountains on the other side of the valley. As she drew nearer to them, she was forced to confess what had been obvious to her from the start. There was no sign of a pass opposite. Indeed the slopes ahead of her were steeper than those she had flown over and continued high above her. The air was already thin, she could not risk going higher. Whether this was the correct valley or not, there was obviously no way she could fly out of it.

She allowed the balloon to descend slowly. As she dropped below the level of the pass behind her, she fell into a different air stream. As she hoped, cold air was rolling down the mountains and flowing down the valley. Her balloon started to drift steadily south.

Soon she was starting to see signs of humanity. A string of pack ponies heading north along the valley; smugglers going to deal with the lichen gatherers?

In the valley bottom there were trees, admittedly not many, but it was a start. As she continued south there were first, the scattered shielings of the shepherds, and then the small farms, crofters wrestling a living out of a hard land. Finally in the distance she saw a complex of buildings. As she grew closer she could see orchards, enclosed fields, farms and finally, surrounded by trees, the recognisable pinnacle of a shrine. If she hadn't found 'the' monastery, she had at least found 'a' monastery.

Slowly she allowed the balloon to descend. It came to rest with a slight bump and Maljie somewhat stiffly climbed out of the basket and stood once more on firm ground. It occurred to her that, as she considered her flight, she had done more ridiculous things, but not recently and rarely while wearing clothes.

Already there were lay brothers running towards her from the monastery. She pulled herself together and waited until the first of the young men had started to slow his pace to a walk. "I need to speak to Hegumen Sydna, or failing that the Claustral Prior." She racked her brains to remember the latter's name. "Father Goodwill."

The lay brother gestured wordlessly at the deflated balloon.

Maljie said, "And I'll need a horse and cart so I can gather this up properly and take it inside. So you," she looked round and pointed at the next two lay brothers, "You and you, stay here, stop anybody walking on it and make sure it doesn't blow about." She set off walking towards the monastery. Her course intercepted that of one of the lay brothers who was older and slower than the others. "And you can take me to Father Goodwill or the Hegumen Sydna." The lay brother stopped and turned to walk alongside her. "Father Goodwill led vigils so he'll be going to breakfast about now. The Hegumen will be leading the morning meditations."

With more enthusiasm than she'd intended, Maljie said, "Breakfast sounds good."

Maljie was led into the monastic enclosure through the main gate. They bore left, between the kitchen and the Abbot's house, her guide pointing out the various buildings as they passed. Then they followed a gravelled path down the side of the infirmary which turned right and led to the refectory. The lay brother opened the door and ushered Maljie in. She was in a long room with perhaps a dozen polished wooden tables. Only one was occupied. Seated at it, eating thick porridge and engaged in sporadic conversation were two men, one of them quite young, and a woman, the incumbent Maljie had travelled to meet. The incumbent looked up. "Maljie, what in the forty-seven non-canonical hells are you doing here?"

"We have a problem."

The older of the two men gestured to the waiting lay brother. "I suspect it will be a problem best discussed over breakfast. Fetch our sister a bowl please." He then turned to Maljie, "I am Father Goodwill, the claustral prior."

Maljie turned to study the younger man who started to fidget and looked embarrassed. "You're Jarl Blagfoot, Yaggan Blagfoot's son."

"Yes madam."

"So you're here to smuggle lichen."

The young man said nothing, he realised Maljie had made a statement rather than asked a question.

At this point a bowl of porridge arrived for Maljie. She noted that Jarl's bowl was empty. "So young man, could you run along and do whatever smugglers do when they're not smuggling. I've got something to tell these people."

When the young man had left the refectory, Maljie poured out the whole story, including the rumour that there was a faction which wished to make Hegumen Sydna the next Autocephalous Patriarch.

There was a gratifying silence as Maljie stopped speaking. Then Father Goodwill turned to the incumbent. "It is obvious that you have upset somebody. I'm now wondering whether our Hegumen's prospective translation is part of the same project or an entirely different machination."

The incumbent turned to Maljie. "So how soon do we have to get back to Port Naain to stop this?"

"I wouldn't want to take more than a fortnight."

"So, Father Goodwill, have you any transport I can borrow?"

"I'm sorry, all we have is the Hegumen's palanquin. It is carried by eight lay brothers and I always reckon on it taking four weeks to get to Port Naain."

Maljie said, "Four weeks! I could walk it faster."

"Yes but you'd not be carrying a damned big palanquin."

Maljie stood up, "If you've not got transport, it looks as if I need a quiet word with young Jarl."

Maljie found the young man in the stables. He was rubbing down his two horses. He started when she entered.

Maljie looked at his cart. It was certainly big enough for what she needed. She looked inside where there were a score of large packets wrapped in canvas. As Jarl watched she opened one, stuck her finger in and then licked it.

"Jarl, why did you decide to go into smuggling?" Defensively he replied, "My father was one of the best and I wanted to be better than him."

"Jarl, you've been listening to your grandmother again. A fine woman, a devoted mother. But Yaggan was probably the worst smuggler Port Naain had ever seen. The lichen he supposedly smuggled was warehouse floor sweepings padded out with sawdust he'd stained."

She gestured at the packets in the cart. "This stuff is no more than catering standard but your father never sold anything so good."

"Catering standard?" Jarl sounded shocked.

"Catering standard. Yes it is lichen but the duty on it is so low it's not worth smuggling. I doubt it'll fetch more than three alars a pack in Port Naain."

"But I paid two and half and was guaranteed it as grade three."

Sympathetically Maljie put an arm around his shoulders. "Then you were robbed my boy. Now let Aunty Maljie take charge." She turned to where the lay brother who was supposed to be mucking out the stables leant on his fork, listening to the conversation with obvious interest. "Can you ask Father Goodwill to come down here please?" When he seemed hesitant, she added, "Don't worry, you won't miss anything." When Father Goodwill had arrived, he found Maljie in the cart, having opened all the packages.

She stepped carefully down from the cart. "Father, I assume you're still producing your tonic wine?"

"We are indeed, it's all that keeps us financially viable."

"Wine?" Jarl said incredulously. "How can you produce wine up here?"

Maljie said, "Pulp your apples, press them for the juice, and then boil up the pulp for a day or so. Strain off the liquor and then add one part pure grain alcohol to seven parts liquor. Add a handful of lichen per barrel and store for a year or so. Then bottle and sell."

"It's nearly one part to six, and it's a double handful of lichen but yes, that's about the strength of it." Father Goodwill rubbed a hand through his thinning hair. "We do have standards you know, and a loyal customer base that expects the best."

"And you'll get your lichen direct from the collectors."

"Well it would be damned silly to send to Port Naain from it."

Maljie continued, "And I suspect you'll be able to sort it and put some of the nice stuff to one side."

"We only use grade two, but we do get some grade one that we might release onto the market at some point."

"Right." Maljie gestured at the packages in the cart. "Jarl will trade you these for your grade one. You'll be able to use this, perhaps an extra handful or two per barrel, but it'll see you right. In return he'll transport a load of your tonic wine to Port Naain, free and gratis, as well as my balloon, me and the incumbent."

"And the Hegumen. Abbot Sydna has decided that whatever happens in Port Naain, he doesn't want to miss it."

📖📖📖

The cart made its way carefully out through the gate of the monastery, avoiding the potholes in the track.

Jarl led his horses rather than drove them for this bit, only climbing up onto the driver's seat once they were clear of the gate. Maljie, sitting beside him, was already nodding. Too little sleep was starting to catch up with her. The cart had been nicely packed. It was filled with crates of tonic wine, each crate protected from its neighbours by a layer of straw. One crate, towards the front, on the bottom row, was different. It too was protected by straw, but in the case of this case the protection was cosmetic. The crate contained Jarl's precious packages of grade one lichen.

On top of the crates, two of the lay brothers had laid a shelf of boards and the hegumen and the incumbent perched on these. Also loaded onto the cart was the party's luggage. Maljie was restricted to very little more than she stood up in. Ballooning is not conducive to travelling with a large wardrobe, allowing for multiple changes of dress. Jarl had a blanket roll, the hegumen a slim satchel, and the incumbent had two large chests, mainly containing theology tomes she had acquired at the monastery. The balloon had to remain at the monastery. Father Goodwill managed to demonstrate, even in the face of Maljie's obduracy, that there was no way that you could fit the balloon on top of the load without removing the awning, and this latter action was a step too far for her fellow passengers. So the balloon had been carefully put away in a store room, and one lay brother had been personally taken to one side by Maljie. She had explained to him, in eye-watering detail, what would happen to him if her cherished balloon were to be even slightly damaged. Father Goodwill had cheered her somewhat by pointing out that if she visited next year, the monastery always had a good stock of raw spirit, and it was entirely possible she would be able to fly the balloon home, or explore further depending on her whims and the vicissitudes of wind and weather.

They were perhaps a mile from the monastery when Abbot Sydna looked round and said in jovial tones.

"Isn't this fun, a pleasant smuggling trip in good company?"

"Smuggling?" The incumbent's response was sharp enough to cut through the doze Maljie was slipping into.

"The Abbot mis-spoke, it won't be smuggling until we neglect to pay a toll when we pass through Woodpin." Maljie felt she had summed up the situation nicely, then deftly changed the subject. "I note we haven't got much in the way of supplies with us?"

Abbot Sydna produced a list from his satchel. "Father Goodwill provided an itinerary. If we arrive at these places on time then not only will we be fed and housed but shall arrive in Port Naain in decent time."

Maljie and Jarl studied the itinerary. Maljie said, "But it'll take three weeks."

"Well you said your people would delay the meeting." Maljie sat in silence. Jarl who was also studying the list asked, "What are we to expect from the catering?"

Abbot Sydna leaned forward. "On feast days we will feast, and on fast days we will fast." He leaned back. "It's theological sound."

Jarl persisted. "But how many feasts and fasts?"

"Ah, now you delve deep into the underpinnings of our order. When I was a novice I had to learn by rote the feasts and fasts of the order. Seven hundred feast days and eight hundred and forty seven fasts, three of which depended upon the position of the moons on the day of the fast."

"But there aren't that many days in a year." Jarl protested.

The Abbot turned to the incumbent. "A sharp young man, he spots in an instant an embarrassing detail that took theologians and masters of the lore four hundred years to come to terms with." He turned back to Jarl. "Indeed I had barely finished my noviciate when the Wandering Conclave reported. It had deliberated on the matter for nearly forty years. Finally the Autocephalous Patriarch of the day insisted they moved their meeting to Cold Dregdale.

After a week there, they eventually came to a decision. This reduced the total number of feasts and fasts to four hundred each." He raised a hand, "I know what you're going so say, young man, that there are still too many. But on a day with two or more feasts, or two or more fasts, one merely studies the positioning of the appropriate lesser moon to decide which feast or fast it actually is."

Jarl persisted. "But how do you know whether a day is a feast or a fast?"

"Simple, it is determined by the spirit driven wisdom of the hegumen, incumbent, or suitable appropriate authority." He paused briefly as if considering his statement, "Or perhaps their arbitrary whim, but still, we now have a situation of absolute clarity."

"So," Jarl asked, "What is today?"

"Today is the 'Third ritual mortification of Temple Wardens' which can be regarded as a fast or a feast, but is considered the most auspicious day for erecting a new pillar for a stylite. It is also the 'Commemoration of the Ritual Defenestration of Jagathorn Beale.' He was a distant predecessor of mine and his day is regarded by some parts of the order as a fast and by others as a feast."

Jarl, somewhat bemused, asked, "So will we celebrate a feast or a fast?"

"We spend tonight at the Shrine of Aea in the North. The matrons there are excellent cooks. Declaring today a fast day would be an insult verging on a mortal sin."

📖📖📖

One doesn't so much 'arrive' at Woodpin as realise that Woodpin is somehow coalescing around one. As an aside, I know Woodpin reasonably well. Eventually the formal entrance to the village is marked by a hotel. Coming from one side it is the Woodpin Salutation Hotel. Should you approach from the other side you are met by the Woodpin Grandiloquent Hotel.

The hotels are perhaps two miles apart if that, and all between is the heart of Woodpin. Admittedly the heart of Woodpin does, by this definition, include a lot of field but still one cannot have everything. The exact middle of the village is the farm of Old Bulwin. He has a large barn and has been known to host theatrical performances.

Incidentally both hotels are very similar, they were probably built by the same man perhaps a century or more ago. Both have two rooms which can be rented out to travellers, along with a common room which comfortably seats twenty but will hold thirty if it is summer and everybody is willing to accept greater familiarity than is considered polite in some places. For a traveller, difficulties can arise because the two hotels are owned by two sisters. Both were taught to cook and brew by their mother, so in all honesty there is very little to choose between them. But may Aea have mercy on the traveller who cannot find a score of obvious reasons why 'this' hotel is infinitely superior to 'that' hotel. To be fair, the beer is entirely reasonable and the food more than adequate. Had I not had something of a falling out with one of the sisters I would be happy to frequent either hostelry. Still if one looks on the bright side, whilst one sister will happily lynch me, the other will undoubtedly hug me to her bosom as a long lost brother and pour beer with an unstinting hand.

As our intrepid travellers arrived on the outskirts of the village, you would notice subtle and not so subtle differences in their appearance. Jarl was now dressed in the robes of a lay brother of the order, whilst Maljie had been persuaded to don the robes of a stipendiary maiden penitent. Abbot Sydna seemed to be almost entirely relaxed. He wore the happy air of a man on holiday with good companions.

The incumbent on the other hand wore the somewhat strained air of the person who has come to the uncomfortable realisation that they are, in some respects, the token adult in the party.

As they entered the village, the Abbot felt the need to reminisce about the history of the place. "When I first became Abbot we had problems with communications to Port Naain. On the positive side this meant that we received few of those interminable encyclicals and similar. Indeed for three whole years we went without a single document explaining how we had to update this or that procedure. Unfortunately it meant we couldn't sell our produce, which enables us to buy in various items. We thus had almost total self-sufficiency thrust upon us." He paused, "It wasn't easy but if offered the choice again I might be tempted."

Jarl, used now to his role as the one who had to keep the Abbot and his stories on track, asked, "What was the problem."

The village was being preyed upon by three bandit gangs. One was led by a cunning villain called Brovak, also known as 'bastinado' because he punished those who offended him by beating the soles of their feet in order to break the small bones within. He commanded five men.

Then there was Gruz, a crossbreed with elements of nomad and beastman in his lineage. He was once the lieutenant of Brovak, a huge, shambling brute who commanded by pure fear and lacked all grace of manner. He commanded four men. Finally there was Vavil, a relative newcomer, who led a band of six swaggering bravos. This group was apparently initially from Port Naain and were characterised by fanciful clothing and red, quinquicorn hats, a fashion I am sure I have seen somewhere before."

"Three bandit gangs seems a little excessive for such an area."

"Indeed I would be tempted to agree with you, Jarl.

But you must understand that Woodpin does sprawl somewhat provocatively over quite an area."

"So what happened to them," Maljie asked.

"Kierkel Laikin happened to them. She was an Urlan maiden who was travelling through the area on some errand or another. One of the bandits made a suggestion she considered improper and in the next half an hour apparently she slew all of them. After surveying the heads she only took away that of Gruz for her collection. Apparently her trophy cabinet had expanded into a third room by that point and there was pressure on her to be more selective as to which heads she kept."

"Isn't Kierkel Laikin just some figure of legend?" Maljie asked.

"Oh no, she went on to marry Tarsen Charnkin, he's Baron Rackland, so she now lives in an impressive castle on the southern ocean with a large brood of children, grandchildren too perhaps by now."

Jarl commented, a little sadly, "I've never heard of these people or places."

The Abbot smiled benevolently at him. "Yes but you're from Port Naain, and people from there are notoriously parochial. The Combined order of Aea stretches out across most of the Lands of the Three Seas. I myself crossed the Aphices Mountains as a boy, hitching a lift on a wagon loaded with steel forgings. It had been decided that I showed potential so would do my noviciate in the west."

At the middle of the village was an open square with houses on three sides of it. The fourth side was Old Bulwin's farm and a field where orid grazed. In the centre of the square was an empty gallows, and under the gallows was a small wooden hut. The hut, and the house nearest to it, bore the arms of Lord Cartin. In front of the hut was a table at which sat three rather bored soldiers. One, a sergeant, stood up and walked across to the cart.

"Welcome to Woodpin, the home of all that is good and lovely."

His tone of voice indicated that only the presence of the fair sex prevented him from spitting onto the ground to punctuate his comment.

Maljie looked primly at the sergeant. "Thus are the blessings of Aea distributed to the deserving and undeserving alike."

The sergeant completed the formula, "All praise be to the name of Aea."

Maljie smiled at him. "It is nice to meet somebody who has been properly brought up."

"Learned it on my mother's knee, Mistress." The sergeant's tone became more business-like. "So what are you transporting, we have to collect toll on consignments of lichen."

Maljie gestured at the cart. The incumbent and the abbot carefully moved their robes so that the sergeant could see the crates. "We have nothing but the tonic wine made by the brothers who continue their prayers and devotions even as they work. Thus producing something which fortifies the spirit even as it eases the pains of the body."

She reached inside her robe and the sergeant flinched backwards half a step. Maljie produced a bottle of the tonic wine. "May this warm you against the chill of the morning and sooth the movement of your bowels."

The sergeant made a half bow as he took the bottle. "A benediction on you, reverend maiden penitent." He turned. "Togger, give the lady a chit to say they're clean and not carrying lichen."

The young solder stepped forward and handed Maljie the appropriate piece of paper. She granted him her most benign expression, nodded to the sergeant and gestured to Jarl to put the cart once more into motion.

As the cart disappeared out of the square, Togger turned to his superior. "Sarge, I'm surprised at you falling for the 'just transporting tonic wine' crap."

The sergeant shrugged. "Look, if you want to fall out with Maljie, just do it on somebody else's shift, not mine."

Chapter 8

I suppose it is now time to return to my own travails.
I parted company with Gord Roseban at the door of
his hut and headed once more down the mountain.
Now I had some idea of where I was, and a plan for
getting home. I also had the name of a farmer further
down the mountain who supplied Gord with those
necessities he couldn't grow himself. My hope was to
prevail upon him to assist me further.

My obvious problem was a shortage of financial
assets. However as I descended it was bound to grow
warmer so I felt I could discard my flunky's uniform.
This I rolled up and carried in the basket. The wig I'd
left with Gord. As he explained, he would wear it not
for vanity but for warmth, the nights are chill up
there.

Now I was following a path. Not a well-marked one it
is true but still, it was easy enough to follow. I wasn't
sure how far off the farm was, Gord was vague,
merely commenting he could walk there and back in a
day. I felt that this must mean I would get there
before midday. As it was, I somewhat over-estimated
my ability to bound nimbly along the mountain paths
like a beillie. Still about noon the path finally turned a
corner under the shoulder of the mountain and could
see below me a narrow green valley with a couple of
small farms. As I continued to descend I could see
that the nearest farm had their orids gathered close
to the farm in a series of stone walled pens. It was
obvious that I had arrived in time for shearing.

To get to the farm house I had to walk past the pens,
and a man of my own age was sitting on a pile of
fleeces taking his midday repast.

"Going far brother?"

"Port Naain eventually. But I've just come from
Gord."

"Then you'll be hungry." He stood up and waved
towards the house.

A young woman appeared. "Fetch some lunch for a brother who's come down from visiting old Gord."
I sat down on a pile of fleeces next to him and the young woman fetched me a tankard of small beer and some bread, cheese, slices of cold smoked orid and some pickle. My host introduced himself.

"I'm Farren, this is my daughter Helgi, and my lady wife, Crastine, is inside."

"I am Tallis. I'm trying to get back to Port Naain as there are urgent matters that need attending for the order."

"How were you thinking of getting there?"

"I thought to follow your valley out of the mountains and then just keep walking south. I know the area north of Port Naain reasonably well."

"Well, you'll know that up here we're barely fifteen miles from Sweethaven."

I hadn't realised we were so close, but I still wasn't sure how that helped me. Sweethaven was the northern most village on the coast. North of it the mountains met the sea and nobody travelled any further. Certainly if I had money I could probably get passage south to Port Naain. There again, if I had wings I could fly there.

"We're so far north?"

"You are, my friend. Now I was thinking as how I might be able to do you a favour. Are you too proud to get your hands dirty?

"Well it's a year or two since I trimmed the feet of orids but I was considered a good hand at the time."

"Right, this is my dilemma. Helgi here is supposed to go to Sweethaven to marry a young man who has taken her fancy."

Helgi broke in, "Well I've only known him for twenty years so don't make it sound like I'm wandering off into the wilds in response to an advertisement in a temple newsletter."

Farren ignored her with the casual ease of a man who knows that for once the ladies in his life have to listen to what he has to say.

"Well her mother is in the house frantically trying to 'refresh' a dress for Helgi to be wed in in two days' time. But at the moment I'm trying to get through shearing, and I'm shorthanded, what with Crastine so busy. So I'm going to struggle to get finished clipping before we have to leave for the wedding. If you can stay and give me a hand, when we go down to the wedding, we can take the wool clip and when it goes on the boat to Port Naain, you can travel south with it."

"I never sheared a sheep so I'd better leave that to you, but I can catch them, dag them out, and check feet at the same time."

"Well hopefully Helgi can catch them and check the feet, you dag them out, put them in the race and I'll clip them. He stood up and showed me the way his pens worked. There was a large pen which funnelled into a smaller pen. From the end of the small pen ran a narrow race, just the width of an orid. At the far end was another pen, this one somewhat cleaner and stacked outside the pen was a pile of tightly rolled fleeces.

"Helgi drives them down the funnel, then when the small pen's full, you two check feet, dag them out and put them in the race. I take them out of the race, clip them, roll the fleece and let them back out to grass."

So we set to work. The day was pleasant and both my companions knew their trade. Not only that but the shears I had been handed were sharp. Things went with a swing, and if the sweat ran down my face and into my eyes, I had time to wipe my brow with my forearm before Helgi passed me the next ewe.

Time passed in a blur, then instead of a ewe, Helgi passed me a tankard of beer. "Mother's landed."

I stood up straight and stretched. An older woman was standing with a jug. Like her daughter she was stocky, thick set, and whilst Helgi had her long golden hair knotted behind her head out of the way,

Crastine's was cut short and streaked with grey.
Crastine was also immensely irritated.

"That idiot cousin of mine promised to send me enough cloth for the dress. She's send a bluidy handkerchief, and not a big one."

Farren looked up from his tankard. "So you've not got enough material?"

"No."

I pointed to my basket which sat forgotten at the foot of the wall. "Will the clothes in there be any use?"

Crastine opened the basket and held up the flunkey's jacket and trousers.

"The jacket could work over the dress, and I could use the trousers to make panels to let into the dress."

"Then take them with my blessing."

She smiled briefly in my direction, her mind already busy with measurements, lappets, seams and darts. We drank our beer and got back to work.

📖📖📖

That night, after a thick stew of orid and vegetables, I slept on a mattress besides the banked up fire. Occasionally I would drift awake to hear Crastine muttering to herself as she sewed by the light of a candle. Next day we worked from dawn to dusk. I never left the pen, and only put down the dagging shears when I stopped to eat. As the sun set, we pushed the last ewe through into the race and cheered as Farren clipped her.

By the time we had stuffed the fleeces into great sacks and loaded them onto the farm dray, I was walking as stiffly as an old man. Yet when I scrubbed myself off at the pump I realised my hands, protected by the lanolin in the wool, had suffered very little. I barely remember eating that night, and was asleep as soon as I pulled the blanket over me. I heard nothing that night but next morning I awoke to see my robe drying in front of the fire.

Given I would have been willing to swear that I had still been wearing it when I went to bed, this came as something of a surprise.

Crastine gestured to the robe as she passed me breakfast, coffee and porridge, served in separate bowls. "Cannot have you stinking of orids at our Helgi's wedding."

We hitched two horses to the dray and threw a sheet over the woolsacks in case it rained. Then with Farren and Helgi sitting on the seat, Crastine and I sat on top of the sacks. Before the dray was out of the yard, Crastine was asleep and her gentle snoring accompanied us for the next few hours.

The journey was uneventful, although we did see other families, dressed in their best, loading wool onto their carts prior to setting out. All of them would stop and wave to Helgi.

At Sweethaven we dropped Crastine and Helgi off at the Fish Salter's Arms. The two ladies carried bundles of clothes they would change into. Farren and I took the dray down to the harbour where a boat was loading wool. Ours was loaded on, Farren was given a tally chit and I was promised a berth when it sailed south next morning. Whether the captain and supercargo were impressed by my aura of sanctity or were swayed by my promise to help the cook I'm not entirely sure.

We drove back to the Fish Salter's Arms, handed the horses over to the ostler and went to see where the ladies had got to.

We found them in the common room waiting for us. Helgi resplendent in a dress which reached down to mid-calf. The blue skirt was enlivened by pink inserts and was topped off with the jacket, restyled for the female figure. Helgi herself was radiant. It is a phenomenon I've noticed before. Even the plainest young woman can look lovely on her wedding day. Helgi, far from plain, was no exception.

We walked through town to the school room, which was the largest public space available for hire for such ceremonies. But on our way there were two smaller but equally important ceremonies. One of the houses had a sign over the door, "Wool Broker". There was a wide door leading into the front room, and this was fitted out as a strong room and an office. Farren led us into the room and there we were greeted by the broker in person. He shook hands with us all. He was a plump man of middle years, his face weathered from time spent out-of-doors and his hands soft with lanolin from handling a lot of wool. With some ceremony, Farren presented his tally chit.

The broker took it and examined it as if he'd never seen one before. "Terrible bad trade for wool this year."

"Don't tell me that those rogues down in Partann have stopped stealing each other's' orids and have started shearing them instead? Farren's tone indicated that he'd been through this discussion before.

The broker merely said, "And then nobody wants the coarser grades of wool in Port Naain anymore."

I took an opportunity to join in, "Heavy carpeting is becoming fashionable once more, and a lot of ladies who used to boast about their polished wood flooring have grown tired of elderly matrons doing the splits or otherwise being inconvenienced."

The other two looked at me with surprise. The broker said, "You've been teaching him."

Farren had a look of honest surprise, "As Aea is my witness, Saman, he came up with it all by himself. It might even be true."

Saman the broker shook his head sadly, "If people start bringing truth into it, what's a humble broker going to do?"

From behind me Crastine muttered loudly enough to be heard in the street, "Pay up?"

Saman looked at the tally again. "Forty alars."

That was a lot of money. It was forty weeks wages! An honest poet could live for over a year on that. Even I could make it last six months and not feel particularly frugal.

Farren sighed, "I was expecting fifty."

Saman also sighed, even more theatrically than Farren had. "Would that my aged mother was still alive, so that I had something left to sell to help pay these exorbitant prices."

He obviously noticed Helgi, "Anyway, the man who can dress his beautiful daughter in such finery must surely be find it in his heart to accept forty-two alars.

"I'm getting married today, Saman."

The broker's demeanour changed, "Who to? Young Bovington?"

"Yes, we've got a tenancy of a farm owned by a local fane."

"Well I wish you both every happiness." That at least sounded sincere. Then he added, "And remember me when you've wool to sell."

He turned back to Farren. "Forty alars and five to the bride as a wedding present."

Farren held out a hand, "Done."

Saman clasped his hand. "I no doubt have been. Still if I'm lucky I might get a kiss off the bride."

Helgi stepped forward and planted a kiss on his cheek. "And remember to drop in to see us when you're doing your rounds and looking to see what the wool clip will be. I bake scones as well as my mother. And I know all her jam recipes."

Saman laughed and went back to his desk. He counted out money into two piles and gave the larger to Farren, then passed the smaller to Helgi. "Young Bovington is a lucky young man. I hope you'll both be very happy."

As Farren ushered his family out of the officer he glanced back over his shoulder, "If you're free this evening, you might want to join us in the Fish Salter's Arms. Just a bit of supper with a few friends and a chance to drink the health of the bride and groom before they ride off to their own farm to start their new lives together."

☐☐☐

The next visit was a small lawyer's office. By the front door was a wooden plaque. The engraved name, 'Halgast Alwight, lawyer,' was picked out in gold lettering. Again it was the front room of one of the houses along the cobbled street.

As he entered, Farren announced, 'Rent day, Master Alwight."

The lawyer pulled out a ledger and opened it. He ran his finger down the page. "Farren Tuckerway, one tenth of the wool clip, no more than five alars."

"Forty alars for the wool clip, so here are the four I owe you." He pushed the coins across the desk.

The lawyer, an elderly man who sported a wig almost identical to the one I'd left up in the mountains with Gord Roseban dropped the coins into a strongbox bolted to his desk. "As always a pleasure to do business with you Master Tuckerway."

He then stood and bowed to Helgi, "And congratulations on your forthcoming nuptials, Mistress. I wish you every happiness. And my lady wife informs me that she will drop off one of her celebrated fruit cakes at the Fish Salter's Arms. A wedding isn't complete without fruit cake."

Helgi gave a little curtsy back. "I hope you and your lady wife will stop by and drink our health later today."

The old lawyer resumed his seat, then added, "I wasn't asked to draw up your tenancy agreement. Apparently Father Nattan, the Priest, has taken to doing his own. It might be wise to read it before signing. Amateurs make the silliest mistakes."

Helgi nudged her father and hissed, "Remember to check."

Nodding benignly, Farren led us on down the street.

Twice we stopped at shops, one an ironmonger, one a provision merchant, and Farren paid off the annual account. Then it was on to the schoolroom.

There were perhaps a score of people present. Farren and I went in, Helgi and her mother waited in a small side room, so they could make a grand entrance when everybody had arrived. Father Nattan, a priest of Aea Unreconciled, a man who had run to flesh, studied the lesser brevity as he stood by a table at one end of the room, a pile of papers in front of him. I would have been more impressed with his display of piety if he hadn't been holding the book upside down. I assumed he was using as a shield as he read something else.

Farren led me to the table, introduced me to the priest but also to the two other men who were standing there. One was Young Bovington, the other his father. I examined the younger man out of the corner of my eye. Having worked closely with Helgi I'd got a lot of time for her and hoped she was marrying somebody who would appreciate her. I was reassured by what I saw. A young man who obviously scrubbed up reasonably well, he still had the look of somebody who wasn't afraid of hard work. His father too looked like he spent his life outside in all weathers.

Father Nattan gestured to the papers on the table, "Farren, here is the marriage contract, the tenancy contract and this is the notification of marriage I'll send to Port Naain when I fill it in."

The latter document I recognised, I'd seen plenty of them. The other two were new to me, and out of habit I picked them up. Some of this is because I'm a poet, I cannot avoid reading things. I will stop and look at public notices, checking the scansion. You never know when something will either provoke a verse or drop into one already half formed. Then as a very junior temple warden, I'd had it drummed into me that you always look at things before you sign them.

The marriage contract was standard, I've written up a dozen of them. The tenancy contract on the other hand was entirely new to me. I found myself nodding along to the cadence of ancient formulae, the rights of graziers, the keeping of orid tups in well fenced pastures, the need to maintain buildings and keep the land in good heart. I suspected these paragraphs had changed little over the centuries. Then I came to the rent. "One fifth of the wool clip, no less than five alars."

I nudged Farren, who was deep in conversation with Old Bovington. "Is this usual. It's a lot more than you're paying."

He casually read the line, then took the document off me, read the line again and thrust it at Old Bovington. "You seen this!"

Old Bovington turned on the priest. "You thieving 'ook. What you playing at?"

Father Nattan turned and obviously intended to bestow a lofty gaze on the older man but was forced to recoil to avoid being hit in the face by the tenancy agreement.

This obviously upset the priest's equilibrium because he too raised his voice. "Behave yourself sir or there will be no marriage and no tenancy."

"You threatening us?

"No, I'm just telling you what will happen." The priest had recovered his courage.

"What's going on?" Helgi, resplendent in her bridal finery, had obviously overheard the shouting and followed closely by her mother, was storming across the room to find out what was happening."

It was Young Bovington who answered. "Bastard is trying to gouge us for rent and threatening to cancel the wedding if we don't pay."

Helgi made a bee-line for the priest. Her father and future father-in-law both stepped out of the way. The priest tried to barge past her but he had misjudged his woman.

The previous day I had seen Helgi sidestep an orid tup charging at her, and with a well-timed grab and pull had put it on its back ready to check its feet. Given that the tup would weigh as much as some men, it was a feat worth seeing. Now it was the priest's turn. As he pushed past she caught his shoulder, spun him round and when he went down she placed a foot firmly in the middle of his chest to hold him there.

She leaned forward and stared him in the eye, "Well if this worm won't marry us, I've got my own priest. Father Tallis here will marry us. And we'll sign the tenancy, but with the usual rent."

The priest started to say something but she just put her weight on his chest and he changed his mind.

I took the contract and looked at it. My mind was racing. Very junior temple wardens cannot even conduct marriages in their own temple, unless there are certain very extenuating circumstances. The bride standing on the priest and refusing to let him move or speak wasn't one of the circumstances the regulations mentioned, but they did allow for flexibility. Hopefully there would be flexibility enough. Also if I altered the tenancy agreement and it was signed and witnessed then it too might be legal enough.

I carefully altered the section on the rent expected. I then added an addendum explaining there was an error in the initial document and got everybody present to sign the addendum. Crastine took over the role of standing on the priest whilst her daughter and future son-in-law signed the tenancy agreement.

I then picked up the text of the marriage service and called everybody to order. This meant that the priest was left unattended. He scrambled to his feet and made for the door. At the door he stopped, "I'm off to Port Naain, I'll get the marriage annulled and I'll get your Father Tallis unfrocked."

'Good luck with the last bit', I thought. Then in my most mellifluous tones, I started to recite the liturgy.

Chapter 9

The trip home to Port Naain was remarkably trouble free. A Sweethaven wedding, whilst not exactly temperate, is really just a few family friends dropping round for a drink and a bite to eat. So whilst drink was most definitely taken, I managed to make my way to the boat unaided. Given I was carrying a tray of meat pies for the crew, this was fortunate.

I arrived at Port Naain on the morning tide, it was barely daylight. Given the state of the tide I knew Shena, my lady wife, would not be in her office for a few more hours. So I stopped at a one of the barbers who set their chairs out on the side of the ropewalk. There I had my hair trimmed but more importantly I had a shave. Normally when travelling I will take a razor with me, so on this occasion, whilst not 'fiercely bearded' I had the makings of a full set. Now I confess I have shunned facial hair. Not only is Shena not keen on it, but I have a duty to my patrons. Many of them are older than me. They are wise ladies who in their comparative youth, spotted my prodigious potential talent and took me under their wing. Now for any number of years, I was introduced as the charming young man they discovered. I can hardly appear in their houses, grizzled and obviously a man full of years and wisdom, without giving the lie to their claims that they are barely middle aged.

So looking suitably dapper, especially given I was still wearing the mendicant's robe and sandals, I made my way back to the barge. As I thought, Shena was there and together we breakfasted on mott bacon I had acquired from the Purser before leaving the boat that morning. Properly dressed and gradually becoming used to trousers and shoes, I told her the tale of my adventures. After she'd listened she suddenly commented, "Oh, that new Deacon of yours was down at the Old Esplanade."

That surprised me. "What was he after? Wood?"

"No, sand, or at least sandy mud."

Given then amount of salt and other less desirable ingredients that can be found in the mud of the estuary, he wasn't going to use it to make mortar.

"Perhaps he's bedding up a few plants and has some that need the salt?"

"A few? He collected three cart loads of sand. He had the mendicants loading it, but with the shore-combers watching to make sure he took nothing of value."

The shore-combers are very protective of the mud of the estuary. Aea have mercy on somebody who takes some without them checking it first.

"What does he want three cart loads of mud for?"

Shena shrugged. "I don't know and he didn't really say. I just wondered if you would know."

Then she went down to her office at the Old Esplanade and I looked through the scant messages I had received. In all honesty it didn't look as if I had been missed much. Summer is often a quiet time, but surely, when the leading poet of his generation leaves the city, somebody should notice?

Still two or three patrons had sent me notes requesting my attendance. Fortified by my breakfast I set off to visit them.

The first to be visited was a considerably older lady. When her daughter, son-in-law and grandchildren decamped to the countryside every summer, she would always announce that rural living played havoc with her aches and pains, and she would stay in Port Naain to ensure that the servants didn't plunder the house and leave them penniless.

The day her daughter left the premises, she first got the servants to swear on their lives that they would look after the old harridan. As daughter walked out of the door, the old lady would contact me. I would meet her in the front parlour, where accompanied by the butler and housekeeper, (who were utterly devoted to her) we would plan a series of entertainments.

These would involve ladies of her age who had also managed to evade magisterial instructions from daughters who 'know what is best.'

The days would start with a light luncheon perhaps an hour after noon, and then there would be a programme of various entertainments, put on at dignified intervals to allow plenty of time for discussion between the performances. There would be a light evening meal, three small courses but everything exquisitely prepared, because at that age you don't want large meals.

After dinner there would be dancing, or cards, or perhaps both. The occasional surviving husband from the era would of course be invited, as would those widowers who had been part of the circle in the past, plus gentlemen admirers from days gone by. All in all they were a very pleasant occasion and I always enjoyed organising them.

The next patron was a lady in middle years. Her husband, an established usurer, generally liked and respected, had reached a significant birthday. Now normally these are organised in some of the larger restaurants or those public halls where they offer catering. But my patron had in mind something different. Because it was summer and so many wives and families were out of the city, it would be a smaller, private affair in their dining room. Her plan was that the guests, the close friends of her husband, could if they wished, fetch their mistress or equivalent.

Her concept was that it was her husband's party, and he was quite a shy man, but one who had gathered around him a number of close friends, all male, and from a variety of backgrounds. So seated around the table would be two other usurers, a jockey, two condottieri, a theatre critic, a violin maker and a specialist glass blower.

Her plan was to ensure there were enough ladies present to ensure proper decorum, but not so many that they dominated the proceedings and so the gentlemen would be able to discuss matters of mutual interest, be they interest rates, the difficulty of getting really good horsehair, or the prospects of the latest acquisitions made by various stables.

As you can imagine, this promised to be an interesting evening, and knowing her husband's tastes in music and verse, one I could easily organise. The third was somewhat different. I was contacted by Decan, the manager of the Misanthropes. I confess to being intrigued as to what he would want of me. I arrived at his office in the middle of the afternoon and he was so genuinely pleased to see me he called for wine from his private store. As I sipped appreciatively at my glass he explained his problem. Apparently as a purely commercial enterprise it had been decided to hire Melton Renam to produce a banquet. Drawn by the magic of the name, (for at the time he was probably one of the two or three leading cooks in Port Naain or Partann) people would pay for tickets. The resulting profit would help balance the books, as various other customers had been slower than usual at settling their accounts.

I stopped him. "This is interesting but I'm not sure where I come in. You've a score of poets upstairs who'll perform purely for a seat at the table."

Decan ran his fingers through his long dark hair. "Because I don't need a poet, I need somebody I can trust."

Well that rather shook me. He continued, "Tallis, every so often I look at your tab and wonder whether you've been entertaining Sinecurists and their mistresses. At one point I wondered whether you'd used us to fund the overthrow of a Partannese lordling. But you eventually pay it off."

I must confess my tab had got a little out of hand. It had started innocently enough, but then I discovered I could buy decent wine, by the bottle, over the bar, more cheaply than some of my patrons could get it from the wholesalers.

So when I organised events for them, I bought the wine from the Misanthropes. At one point I had to send a dray pulled by four horses to collect my order from the bar. Eventually my patrons remembered to pay me, but Lancet Foredecks caught sight of my bar tab at the time and lauded it as one of the finest pieces of performance art he'd ever witnessed.

"I'm flattered, Decan, but what do you want me to do?"

"When we hire Melton, the food is excellent and people pay high prices, but his ingredients cost us a fortune."

"The best ingredients aren't cheap."

"Tallis, last time he worked here, the wine he was using for cooking came from a Bassman's Spur vineyard."

"Which one?"

"The Foiled Taxman. And the wine was from the year of the Double Salvation."

"But that stuff is an alar a bottle."

"Our cellar here has three bottles. It's a truly beautiful wine. Yet Melton purchased twenty bottles from his supplier to marinate meat in."

I sat in stunned silence. Decan continued. "Apparently he's twisted his ankle so he asked if I could provide him with an assistant to do the fetching and carrying. So I wondered if you could act as a kitchen drudge and watch him for me please."

I like Decan. After all, who else would have let me run up that sort of bar tab without demanding the keys to the barge as security? "Certainly Decan. I'd be delighted to help out."

◫◫◫

After speaking to Decan I felt that I perhaps ought to drop round at the Shrine to Aea in her Aspect as the Personification of Tempered Enthusiasm. After all, it struck me as only sensible to go and see what was going on.

As I arrived in Exegesis Square I could see that a considerable building project was underway. Initially I thought that work had started on the house for Archhierophant Battass Droom but as I pushed through those idlers with nothing better to do than stand and watch, it was obviously not a house. Our idiosyncratic deacon was overseeing the construction. I finally gave in to curiosity and asked him what it was. He broke off from shouting instructions to a mendicant dangling from a rope high above us and said, "It's a stylite's pillar or style. We've got a mendicant who feels that he's being called to be a stylite. I went a little closer and examined the construction more diligently. Imagine a heavy timber base fastened to the ground with long bolts. Then rising up vertically from this base there were two timber pillars. Each was composed of several heavy planks bolted together. Between them was a ship's mast, held vertically by two great steel bolts. The top one was bolted and ostentatiously slathered in grease. The bottom one wasn't fastened and had a handle at one end. At the bottom of the mast there was a large timber box. I had discovered where the estuary mud had gone, the box almost certainly held all three carts full. Interestingly the box didn't in fact touch the ground as the ground had been dug out a little to allow the box to hang free.

The Deacon appeared at my elbow. "It's a damping mechanism, helps to keep things stable." As I nodded wisely he pointed at the two bolts. "The bottom one slides out in case we need to lower the mast."

High above us a group of dangling mendicants were trying to lower a platform onto the end of the mast. The Deacon continued, "The platform will have a bit of a tent on it in case of really bad weather, but nothing too elaborate." Then he seemed to remember himself, "Oh, you're back. Where's Maljie?"

"Somewhere in the mountains. We needed to lose weight to get over the pass, so I've walked home."

"You better find Laxey, he's got a plan but I think he needs help."

I made my way into the shrine to find Laxey working through a great pile of papers. I watched him work his way through the heap. So engrossed was he in his work he never noticed me. He would skim each document, write a couple of questions across the bottom of it, and then return it to the sender seeking further clarification. Within minutes he'd disposed of a whole sack full of paperwork and had effectively done nothing. He looked up and saw me watching him.

"Where in all the hells did you spring from?"

"The balloon was too heavy, I had to walk home. Before you ask I don't know where Maljie and the incumbent are."

Laxey shook his head sadly at the incompetence of the world. "So it looks as if we're going to be forced to delay the conclave. Luckily I've got a plan. It seems that four days before the conclave, the hierophants gather together at the Shrine of Aea Reimagined. Do you know it?"

"I think that it's south of the River?"

"Yes. Apparently they have four days of fasting and silent retreat then on the last day they finish off with a formal meal prepared by one of the better cooks brought in for the purpose. I thought we'd do something with the meal."

"You'd not going to poison the combined hierophants?"

"No, there's no need, we merely need to give them food poisoning. If they daren't go more than twenty yards from the jakes, they're not going to walk in solemn procession to the city to take part in the conclave."

To be fair to Laxey, it sounded a good plan and one entirely within our capabilities. Not only that but I could see no part in it for me. So I felt entirely happy with it. Then Laxey went and spoiled it.

"Of course there's no way I can be seen within miles of place or they'll immediately suspect us.

But you, in your kitchen porter guise, can breeze right in and contaminate the appropriate dish."

"How am I just going to breeze in?"

"Apparently a lot of people gather to pray for the success of the conclave. Just wear your kitchen porter's garb under a long coat."

📖📖📖

With this I made my way back to the barge. Actually I felt somewhat reassured by the turn of events. Given I was the one who was to do the dirty work, others would make it their business to ensure I was in the right place at the right time. Therefore I could dismiss it from my mind and get on with providing joy to my patrons.

For my first patron I decided to call upon Hetti Midton. She is a fine actress, established in her profession and perfectly capable of playing a wide range of parts. But because, unlike a lot of younger actresses, she's passed the stage of wearing tight dresses and making calf-eyes at directors, roles do not come her as regularly as her skills would deserve. But she would be perfect for my patron and her friends. I also found a couple of older musicians who were willing 'to come out of retirement' for a day. Which really means they would rearrange a few lessons and have a day making music rather than spend it listening to a pupil murdering it.

Hetti can deliver my work at least as well as I can, and some of my poems work best with two voices. Also, like me, she can sing a bit without embarrassment although neither of us would claim to be singers. Added to this, she is a good solid professional, easy to work with, and more importantly she has a sense of fun which she can indulge on occasions like this. I had no doubt my patron and her guests would be entirely happy with the entertainment provided.

We would perform, then shut up, join them in conversation (even with the musicians they would have friends in common or stories they could share) and then perform a bit more. Indeed it proved to be one of those days one looks back on with a certain fondness. Our patron not merely paid before we left (important when you're hiring musicians) but kissed us all, (including the musicians) and demanded that we be available at short notice later in the year when her daughter was planning to accompany her husband on a 'business trip' to Oiphallarian.

The second matron's event needed more subtlety. My role was different. Yes I had to deliver a couple of pieces (a piece of comic verse about racehorses and the ladies who back them, and another rather more sentimental poem on true love) but they were as much the ostentatious reason for me being present. My real work was keeping the conversation flowing, diverting it when it flowed into potentially difficult areas, lightening it when it started to get too heavy, and bringing in those who seemed to be saying little. To be frank, it seems such a little thing when you see it done properly, but it is harder work than working. I was drained by the end of the evening but my patron was entirely happy with the way the evening had gone.

This left me free to concentrate on my third patron. I arrived at the appointed time at the Misanthropes in my porter's garb and was shown into the kitchens. Here I immediately adopted a pose of slack-jawed ignorance. Now I have known many kitchen porters. Some of them have, like me, been persons of wit and intelligence who just need the money. I've talked, in the scullery, to people who had written learned papers on topics beyond my comprehension. But the minute somebody else entered the scullery, we reverted to conversing in grunts.

A lot of cooks seem personally affronted if a kitchen porter appears to have any intelligence whatsoever and if you're suspected of being able to read and write they'll make your day hell before dismissing you without pay at the end of it.

When I arrived in the kitchen Decan was talking to Melton Renam and a lady I discovered to be Madam Hestia Renam. Decan didn't so much as introduce me merely point to me and described me as Blot. Melton was sitting in a chair with his leg up on a cushion. He looked at his wife. "You take Blot and get the stuff we've ordered. Then when you're back I'll hopefully be able to make a start."

I followed the lady out and there was a horse and cart tethered outside the kitchen of the Misanthropes. She gestured for me to climb into the back, took the reins, and we set off at a fair clip.

Our destination was Maggin's. Grandfather Maggin was a wine merchant. His son branched out into a wider range of drinks, and his two daughters expanded even further into speciality foodstuffs. The grandchildren range across Domisa hunting down the rare and toothsome. So at Maggin's not only can you get the finest wines, but you can get Urlan plum brandy that was produced by an Urlan, smoked breast of white ulanger, marinated bilk worms (and not the inferior yellow variety), as well as six different sorts of Colbig Wheel cheeses, a yard across and two hand-spans deep. They even have Madame Ghorramagam's Portentous Pickle.

Madam Renan consulted a list, and crates, barrels and sacks were produced and loaded onto the cart. Once we were loaded, Madam signed the ticket and we set off once more. This time we made our way through rather less frequented side streets until we were parallel to Ropewalk. We turned down a back street and Madam halted the cart and gestured for me to dismount and open the double doors. This I did and stepped aside as she brought the cart into a large backyard. True to my kitchen porter's persona I stood by the doors until I was told explicitly to close them and then come and help unload.

I was obviously in a restaurant storeroom. I emptied the cart, placing things where I was told. I finally stacked a crate of Charmer's Enclosure, year of the Maiden's Revenge, to be told to take another crate, also Charmer's Enclosure, year of the Maiden's Revenge, and take it back to the cart. In the true mindless manner of kitchen porters everywhere, I merely obeyed orders. In theory the cart was now filled with identical items to those I'd unloaded, but the stuff I'd loaded had been standing in the storeroom. At one point Madam Renan left me to my work and disappeared into the front of the building. I took the chance to look round. There were a score of crates of empty wine bottles, all fine vintages. They were next to three wine barrels set up on their stands. Below the tap of one was a jug and a funnel. Madam called me and I went through the door she'd left by. I found myself in a short corridor. Off to one side was a cold room. Madam was peeling the breasts off common domestic fowl and placing them in a keg marked, Maggin's Ulanger Breasts. She replaced the top of the keg and gestured for me to carry it to the cart.

The cart now loaded to her satisfaction I was sent to open the doors and she drove the cart out into the back street. Now on our way back to the Misanthropes, Madam felt less need to stick to quiet side streets. She turned out of the backstreet and made her way down the front of the houses and shops we'd seen only from the rear. Pride of place on the street was a high quality dining establishment, above the window the owner had placed the name in polished ormolu. 'Melton and Hestia Renam, restaurateurs.'

Back at the Misanthropes I was set to unloading the cart. Then under Melton Renam's guidance, his wife and I started preparing the meal. Let us be fair to Melton at this point, once the basics had been done, he grabbed a crutch, stuck it under one arm and hobbled round the kitchen chopping and stirring.

On the grounds that I am being fair to him, I have to admit that not only was he a most accomplished cook, but he was not bad to work for. He never swore at me once and whilst he did throw a skillet at me, I was probably not giving my full attention to the pot I was stirring. Eventually Decan looked a little nervously around the door and said that the guests were arriving. Melton asked for the waiters to be sent up and we immediately started plating up.

Eventually as the last courses were being served and I had started on the washing up, Melton came through to the scullery. "Blot, in three days' time, I'm doing a big meal at the Shrine of Aea Reimagined, South of the River. I'll need a kitchen porter and will you be able to work for me? You can meet us at our restaurant and travel down with us in the cart."

"Yeah."

I managed to infuse my reply with an element of enthusiasm.

"Good."

With that he went back into the kitchen and I kept scouring pans.

Chapter 10

I suppose that I could well have been placed in a moral dilemma. I had been offered the perfect opportunity to enter the Shrine of Aea Reimagined. On the other hand, I had discovered that Melton was cheating his clients, amongst whom was Decan. I could ask Decan to wait a few days before he bearded Melton about the matter, but I wasn't sure I could rely upon Decan to wait that long. It was then that I had the brainwave. All Decan had at the moment was the evidence of a poet.

Admittedly we're not actually banned from testifying in a court of law, but it has to be said that magistrates have been known to adopt a somewhat hurtful attitude to our evidence.

Merely because you can make words rhyme doesn't automatically mean that you have only a casual grasp of reality. Admittedly there are poets who haven't the sense to come in out of the rain, but the same can be said of lawyers and night soil collectors. I would explain to Decan what I'd discovered but recommend that he book Melton for another event and have reliable people burst in upon the guilty couple as they drove their cart load of substituted goods away from their storeroom. That way, Decan could have persons of unquestioned honour among his witnesses. Political figures, those making a living selling property, horse dealers and similar. (And no, I am not bitter about society's attitude to poets.)

I am glad to say that Decan listened to my evidence, and took on board my suggestion of booking Melton Renam again. That little matter dealt with, I then went to give Laxey the good news. I found him in Exegesis Square trying to calm the passions of some of the locals. Apparently the erection of the style with integral stylite had not been an entirely welcome development.

It seems that our Deacon, (strangely absent during this contretemps) had overlooked the fact that most stylites prefer locations somewhat distant from the rest of humanity. This means that they are never accused of using their elevated position to peer in through people's bedroom windows. These accusations were being shrieked at high volume. The aggrieved lady, brandishing the sort of small hatchet one uses for splitting kindling, was threatening to cut down the style and then take her implement to the stylite. The stylite wasn't making things any better. Recently promoted from mendicant, he still had the mendicant's grasp of the coarser byways of language. Eventually one of the interested bystanders asked just who the lady in question had been sharing her bedroom with, given that she was not merely unmarried but had taken it upon herself to police the morals of the area in a stern and unforgiving manner.

She rounded on him, gesturing wildly with the hatchet, but then a younger woman, anonymous at the back of the crowd, commented that she wasn't with anybody, it was just that the stylite had mistaken her putting a nightgown on for two people making love in a sack.

At this point the lady in question realised that the audience were not with her and she allowed Laxey to mollify her with promises that a screen would be erected around that particular part of the style to guarantee her privacy.

She left, still gesturing upwards with her hatchet. The stylite made a rude and distinctly unclerical gesture in return.

As Laxey walked back into the shrine I decided it was now safe to make my presence known. As I told him what I'd achieved he brightened visibly.

"That's the first good news I've had all day, Tallis. Come and look at the meat I've found to add."

With that he led me into the small broom cupboard he uses as an office. The argument he tends to deploy is that his office has no desk, no shelves and nowhere to put papers. Hence it is obvious that his role does not include paper work. Obviously there is the issue that given his office has a plenitude of brooms, brushes and similar, it must include a lot of brushing. Laxey is happy enough with that interpretation. He feels as well qualified to lean on a broom and daydream as the next idler.

He reached behind his brooms and pulled out a bucket. Below the surface of the water there was a piece of meat. Well I assume it was meat, because whilst it was green, maggots rarely infect lettuce. Laxey said, "I've got it under water because otherwise the smell is a bit strong."

"Well I've no doubt it would give anybody food poisoning, but I can hardly sit in a cart with Renan and his wife, carrying a bucket of rotting meat."

Laxey pondered my entirely reasonable comment.

"Well we could have one of the mendicants slip it to you when you're in the shrine."

"It'll have to be properly minced up. Also it'll need something to disguise to scent and flavour."

"What would you suggest?"

"Reconnaissance. I think Shena and I will have to visit Melton and Hestia Renam, Restauranteurs, have a meal there, and contemplate the spices he normally uses."

"That seems sensible. But won't he recognise you?"

"Never in the history of catering has a cook ever recognised a kitchen porter who is off duty."

"Well it seems like a good idea."

"There is one minor problem." I held out my hand, "Thanks to the time I've spent working for the shrine, I'd struggle to afford to buy a pie from a street vendor for Shena and I to share. It strikes me that this is a legitimate expense."

Like a man shedding his life's blood, drop by drop, Laxey put coins into my hand.

📖📖📖

It has to be confessed that Shena and I rarely dine out at anywhere even remotely fashionable. So we did make an effort. Shena, her hair freshly cut, wearing a dress refreshed specifically for the occasion, looked, in my eyes at least, stunning. I would like to think that I managed to keep up appearances. The britches were almost new when the previous owner had died and his widow had summoned me to help disperse the wardrobe.

The silk socks I wore to go with them had never been worn, her late husband was one of these poor unfortunates cursed with unimaginative relatives who unthinkingly give that sort of thing as presents. The jacket was from the wardrobe of another patron.

In this case the husband was still living. He'd seen me standing carefully with my back to the wall so that people wouldn't realise how worn my jacket collar was. He'd quietly whisked me away and had given me this one, which he'd bought but realised it wasn't him. As it was I thought it suited me well enough. Thus you would have thought that as we swept into Melton and Hestia Renams' establishment we were persons of solid substance. Indeed we could have been members of the old aristocracy. The newly rich would be ostentatiously dressed in clothes so new they didn't hang properly. The old aristocracy merely reach into a wardrobe at random and pull out a timeless classic that belonged to a parent or even a grandparent.

A waiter showed us to a table and then explained the menu to us. There was a choice of two starters, either baked river clams, or for the more venturesome, ocean clams served in a rotted seaweed sauce. The fish course was a fish pie, with a choice of Partannese or Toelar style. Then there was but one meat course, loin of orid, marinated in red wine, and then served with salt crust and a hot sauce. Finally for dessert there was a selection of confectioneries, or soured cream plum pie soaked in brandy.

We decided upon a degree of moderation. Both of us had spent too much time on the sands to be overly excited about rotted seaweed. On the other hand we felt that we would gamble on the Toelar style fish pie. Otherwise we would take the meat course and the plum pie. The waiter recommended several wines and we chose a red from Fluance. Given the fish pie we were having, I also ordered two glasses of beer. It is wise to have something on standby when faced with any dish with Toelar in its name.

The meal was excellent. We both enjoyed it, all the more because it was being paid for by somebody else. The use of spices was generous, even with the orid. My suspicion was that the meat was older and rougher than Melton Renam had hoped for and he was doing his best with middling materials. If so, his best was still superb.

Mind you, at one point we heard a crash as something was dropped in the kitchen. This was followed by a clang, the sort of noise one gets if one hurls a pan across a kitchen. It was accompanied by a stream of vituperative abuse which was cut short, probably because the swearer realised he might be heard. Conversationally Shena commented, "It can be so difficult getting good kitchen staff at times.

I had taken the opportunity afforded by the meal to chat to the waiter, discussing the other dishes that might be available should Shena and I visit on a different evening. It was obvious that Melton Renam was fond of using a lot of strong spices. Fortified with this knowledge it was obvious I could be bold when attempting to disguise the flavour of the meat that Laxey had found. Next morning I visited Maggin's as a customer, and enquired about their Devil's Pomatum. Having played host to a friend of mine, Benor, who is a Toelar man, I know more about these things than many in Port Naain. Once he realised I knew what I was talking about, Fildan Maggin, a great-nephew of the founder, was summoned, and he brought with him several packages. One was Blackstrap's Best. Merely opening the top of the jar made our eyes water, but I can remember Benor smearing it on toast and eating it!

Another package contained the seeds of Blackstrap's best. They had been baked and all the cook had to do would be to crush them and sprinkle them on top of the dish of their choice.

The third package was a glass jar containing an oil extracted from the seeds. Fildan Maggin did not remove the stopper explaining that if he did so in an enclosed space, they would have to leave all the doors and windows open for the next two or three days before their building was fit to work in.

I paid him with the last of the coins Laxey had given me, the oil would be perfect for my task.

📖📖📖

I deposited the Devil's Pomatum with Laxey, warned him about the dangers associated with it, and arranged for one of the mendicants to get the treated meat to me when I was working in the Shrine of Aea Reimagined. I then beat a hasty retreat lest he opened the jar, and made my way home. I had an afternoon to work on a project or two of mine own as I didn't have to join the Renan household on their way south until the following day.

Next morning, dressed in my kitchen porter outfit, I appeared at their door and was ordered into the cart. I must confess that had I been a genuine kitchen porter I would have been greatly heartened by my reception. I was not merely greeted courteously but as I took my place in the cart, Madam Renan gave me a breakfast of sausage between two slices of bread. I suspect Shena had been correct, it is difficult to get good kitchen staff and the Renans appeared happy enough to pamper me a little.

At the shrine itself, I was set to unloading the cart whilst Melton Renan, still using his crutch, got to work lighting stoves and setting out the kitchen to meet his exacting standards. I had little time to reconnoitre but did discover that the kitchen is next to the dining room, and both face onto a cloister where pilgrims had gathered to pray for the success of the forthcoming conclave.

On the other side of the kitchen block there was another, lesser courtyard and around that was situated the accommodation of various grades of monks and lay brothers. Indeed some of the novices would use the kitchen as a short cut. These novices were largely children who attended the shrine as much to get an education as because they had any particular calling to the religious life.

At some point in their late teens they would decide whether to continue within the order, or whether to return to the outside world. Thus they were collection of cheerful and largely irreverent imps who doubtless got up to all sorts of mischief and at the same time ensured that their superiors were forced to keep a proper balance between the spiritual and the merely temporal.

I was stationed at the great stove which stood nearest the door onto the cloister. Once Melton Renan and his wife prepared the food, I was the one who would stand and stir it, ensuring all remained under control. But because of the heat of the kitchen I would be instructed to, 'Open that door, we need the draught.' Then five minutes later I would get the shouted instruction, 'Shut that blasted door, there's children all over the place.'

Given that I had a large pan of soup, a whole suckling mott that I was turning on a spit, all the while painting it with gravy and a hot sauce, I was no more put-upon than a kitchen porter would expect. Again, Melton shouted, 'Open the door.'

As I did so a child's hand appeared round it, holding a pottery container. I took it and hastily hid it among some empty jars left by the stove. When the Renans were discussing something complicated I hastily emptied a most of the jar into the soup (Peppered root and orid) and the rest I added to the hot sauce I was painting the mott with. Laxey, or whichever minion he had assigned the task, had done a good job. The meat was chopped so fine it was virtually a paste, and mixed in beautifully. The empty pot I buried in the heap of stuff I would have to wash later. After that brief spasm of excitement, the whole thing went remarkably smoothly. When the gong sounded, Melton Renan and his wife carried bowls of the soup through to the dining room. Then whilst the combined worthies and their advisors were eating that, we put vegetables on plates for them to serve themselves from, and the suckling mott was placed on a large platter so that they could tear their own. I started the process of washing up, something that kept me fully employed until finally I turned round to get another load, only to discover I had finished.

I had just found a broom and was sweeping the floor when Melton Renan and his wife came in from the dining room. They were in high good spirits, their meal had been roundly praised by everybody and Melton paid me then and there. We then climbed back into the cart and returned to Port Naain. By the time I got home I was ravenous. Normally a kitchen porter will find something to eat as he goes along, but in this case I didn't want to eat anything I had prepared.

⏏⏏⏏

Next day I dropped in at the Staircase Shrine about noon. There was an air of suppressed excitement. Everybody was waiting from a message from Laxey, to let us know how our plan had worked. The general feeling was that at some point in the morning there would be an announcement postponing the procession. Finally a mendicant arrived carrying a message from Laxey.

'The meal had no effect, all hierophants are in the best of health and the programme is unchanged.'

That took the wind out of our sails with a vengeance. Finally our Idiosyncratic Deacon looked round the group of us standing despondently around the doorway. "Right, there's nothing for it, we'll have to use my plan after all." He turned to Old Prophet Weldun. "You get yourself to the Office of the Combined Hierophants of Aea."

The old prophet actually grinned, impishly, "Doom, the curse of Aea, feel her wrath!"

It was the Deacon's turn to grin. "Yes."

Weldun almost skipped as he made his way across

Exegesis Square. The Deacon turned to the rest of us. "Right, I want every mendicant in the square in ten minutes, we've got work to do."

He looked up to where the stylite was peering over the edge of his platform. "And you can come down as well. Attach the rope and drop it down to us. And for Aea's sake do it properly or we'll all be in trouble."

I stood back as the square started to fill with mendicants. The last time I saw them so engaged and enthusiastic, we had had to offer free beer. A heavy rope was dropped down from the top of the style and the stylite climbed down it. Then the Deacon stood on the heavy wooden base and started shouting orders. "Right, all of you, get the work. Yes all of you does include you, we've got no innocent bystanders."

He waited until we all had a grip on the rope and shouted, "Now, gently."

As we started to take the strain he grasped the handle of the bottom bolt and tugged. As we pulled we took the weight off the bolt and it slid out. The ship's mast was now suspended on one heavy steel bar that acted as a pivot. "Now pull and keep pulling." We formed two teams, one would pull, and the other would shift their grip on the rope. Then they would pull and the first team would shift their grip on the rope. Slowly and steadily the mast pivoted on the bolt. The great box filled with sand rose high into the air above us whilst the platform on which the stylite lived came down to ground level. At the Deacon's gesture, two mendicants grabbed the platform and tugged. The whole thing had merely sat over the top of the mast, held by its weight, rather than being fastened. We continued to pull and the mast head finally touched the ground. High above us was the box of sand. The Deacon locked a clamp on the rope and then we tied it off securely. He stepped back and watched the mast carefully.

"It's not moving is it?"

I studied it. "A tremor perhaps?"

"Good, now if anybody asks, we're just getting ready

to modify the platform so there is no way our stylite can look into that woman's bedroom window."

"It seems a lot of trouble to go to."

"It is. Now Tallis, could you go and see how our prophet is getting on. I want you back here before dark."

📖📖📖

Now you might well ask, what exactly does a prophet do? After all I have occasionally mentioned Prophet Weldun, but may have been lax when it comes to delving into the role he fulfils. Certainly when I first got caught up in the antics of the Shrine, I too wondered what exactly he did. After all, sitting in a corner, desperately trying to keep an old pipe alight, whilst telling anybody who will listen that everything is going to hell in a handcart isn't normally paid employment.

The pipe I can explain more easily. Old Weldun smokes a mixture of herbs and lichens which are soaked in a mixture of liquids of his own devising. Whilst he claims it produces a smooth and aromatic smoke; because he never gives it time to properly dry, it is a constant struggle to keep it smouldering. The 'hell in a handcart' monologue is also remarkably reminiscent of what you'd hear if you listened to the conversation of any two or three men of his age. In Weldun's case it has to be admitted that the hells mentioned are theologically endorsed and are as described in the Greater Brevity. Indeed even the handcart is hermeneutically sanctioned.

But I realise that I have not yet explained his purpose. Well obviously he serves to remind the young and frivolous that all is not well in the world. He can, if given time, spread a nice aura of vague unease and despondency. Given that he is by nature quite a cheerful chap, one underestimates the effort he has to put into doing this.

But there are times when he has to work more

98

formally. This is where things may become difficult. There are times when a prophet's superiors may suggest he takes a particular line on a subject. There are other times when Aea, whose prophet he is, may well prod him to address a certain topic. I suppose that in some happy instances, both parties are pushing the prophet in the same direction, but in other times this may not necessarily be so. Prophets are a nightmare for bureaucratic organisations, apparently incapable of staying 'on message.' Unfortunately it has been discovered over the years that if the order ignores prophets, Aea merely sends more. Not only that but those she sends tend to be more strident and less reliably housetrained than those we retain.

In times of great formality, when a prophet has a serious message to propound, they will often go back to the very roots of prophecy where the prophet can look uncannily like a tribal shaman.

When I got to the Office of the Combined Hierophants of Aea I could see that Prophet Weldun was in his element. Wearing a kilt of battered sailcloth around his waist, his long grey hair hanging down his back, he capered and gestured and predicted woe. He wasn't alone, there was another prophet there as well. Indeed the two of them seemed to be caught up in a frenzy of competitive doom saying.

A lot of people from round and about had come out to watch them. Street theatre is appreciated by the populace of Port Naain, especially if they don't have to pay for it. I noticed Tiffy standing off to one side and drifted through the crowd to join her.

"What's Prophet Weldun doing?"

Quietly I said, "The Deacon told him to prophesy doom and that is exactly what he's doing. Who is the other prophet?"

"Apparently he's the private prophet of Telbat Spurt, Autocephalous Patriarch."

That rather surprised me. "So what's he doing here?"

"Well the smart money is on him being sent by the Patriarch to try and delay the meeting. Apparently he suspects if it's held now, he'll be demoted."

I watched the two prophets ranting and gesticulating. There was obviously a lot going on I wasn't aware of. This latter point was driven home to me when a third prophet appeared. This one was female, and whilst she wore rather more than the other two, she was not to be outdone in vituperation.

I gestured towards her, "And she is?"

"I don't know." Tiffy looked round, saw somebody and waved to them. A young man came across to join us. "This is Filby, he works on the ground floor." She then addressed the young man, "So who is the woman."

"Eddna, Prophet of the order of Aea Unreformed."

I asked, "So what is she doing here?"

"The order of Aea Unreformed don't recognise the authority of the Combined Hierophants, so they always send somebody to protest at these meetings."

We watched as Eddna produced a bone rattle from somewhere out of her garb and proceeded to dance and gesticulate furiously with it.

Filby spoke with the authority of somebody who had watched rather a lot of this sort of thing. "She is rather good isn't she?"

Prophet Weldun, provoked by her escalation, matched her rattle with two sticks he had stuffed through the belt of his kilt. The Patriarch's prophet produced a ratchet rattle which he held above his head and spun, seeking to drown out the others.

What struck me, as a somewhat anxious observer, was that these were not just general assertions of forthcoming woe. For all the theatrics, these were sharply focussed accusations. The name of Battass Droom came up repeatedly, from all three of them. There again, I suppose the purpose of prophecy is to make the comfortable uncomfortable, and the best way of doing this is often to shine a little light into dark places. I just hoped that somebody knew what they were doing because I had no doubt Battass

Droom would get detailed reports of the occasion and would undoubtedly make his displeasure known.

Filby watched the whole performance with the eye of a connoisseur. "We just need old Borly now. I hope he'll be able to make it."

Tiffy asked, "Who is old Borly?"

"He's an independent prophet, not attached to any particular shrine or order. In fact one of two have accused him of slipping into demonology." Filby's tone brightened noticeably. "Here he is, with his brazier."

Borly was a large man, distinctly portly, and wrapped in a black robe. He set down his brazier and lit it from a fire pot hanging from his belt. The other three moved back, whether to make room for a fellow professional, or to maintain their distance from his brazier wasn't easy to see. Borly himself didn't seem to take a lot of notice of the others, he merely concentrated on his small flame. Slowly a thin column of smoke rose up. As it did so Borly started to chant in a sonorous voice. Much to my surprise the other three joined him in the chant, and drew closer to the brazier. Then Weldun made a complex mystic gesture over the brazier. Three bright flashes of light shot straight up into the sky and everybody fell back. They were certainly dazzling

Weldun fell back so far he was standing next to Tiffy and me. "Right, Tallis. You and I want to be out of here now."

"Do we?"

"Yes." He glanced at Tiffy. "If I were you, I'd think it was time to be going home."

Chapter 11

I arrived back at the shrine and had barely seated myself, never mind tasted the excellent coffee put in front of me when our Deacon appeared. "Could you find Jaysen the night soil collector and tell him I want three carts of night soil, here, just after dark."

Somewhat reluctant to leave my coffee untasted, I took a mouthful and asked, "Doesn't Jaysen take night soil away rather than deliver it?"

I was given the sort of look that Shena will often give me. "Tallis, I've already made arrangements with him. He'll have three cart loads ready for us."

Now I'm a great believer in refreshing one's business model. I know that Jaysen collected night soil and delivered it to farms outside the city. But up until now I'd not been aware of a pent-up demand for it within the city. It's not as if we cannot produce our own.

Our outstanding member of the Idiosyncratic Diaconate glared at me. "Just drink your coffee and then go and tell him."

Well that was a step forward. I smiled my most charming smile. "But of course."

Ten minutes later, suitably refreshed and fortified, I made my way towards Jaysen's yard which at the time was tucked discreetly into the outer edge of Three Mills close to where it meets Commercial and Dilbrook. This of course meant I had to cross virtually the entire city and it was evening by the time I got there. Jaysen was just locking up when I arrived and explained the Deacon's request. He rubbed his hands together with something approaching enthusiasm.

"Right, I've got the carts and even borrowed horses. I'm just a driver short, but you'll do."

Thus I found myself driving a night soil cart through the city. The only words of advice were given to me by Jaysen's lady wife. Jaysen drove the first, I was to drive the second and she would drive the third. As she walked past me she glanced at my cart. "Aye they've overfilled it again. Careful on slopes, it tends to slop about a bit. It's alright going uphill but a bit of a sod when you're coming down."

We wound our way through the city, taking the longer route along the Ropewalk, if only because it is at least level. Night had properly fallen by the time we arrived at the shrine.

Exegesis Square was full of mendicants standing about waiting for something. When we arrived, the Deacon gave orders and a length of sailcloth was laid on the ground under the inverted style.

That done, Jaysen was shouted forward and he drove his cart and unloaded it onto the sailcloth. This was folded over the ordure and the package was then secured by rope to the end of the style which had previously housed the stylite and his platform. Even as this was happening, Prophet Weldun, accompanied by the other prophets, came and clustered round my cart, watching the proceedings. Eddna, Prophet of the order of Aea Unreformed, passed me a beer bottle. "Drink up, Tallis, you're about to see some real cursing."

The Deacon shouted, "Everybody back to the carts." He glanced round to make sure everybody had gone and pulled a lever. This freed the rope which had been holding the styite's end of the style down on the ground. Immediately the great weight of sand suspended high above started to descend. This in turn caused the style to pivot with great speed, flinging the contents of the sailcloth sling off into the night. Old Weldun nodded with satisfaction. "Our Deacon has gone and made himself a trebuchet. He was happy with the final sighting he made on them flashes I sent up. "

I'd read something about trebuchets, siege engines from our relatively distant history, but didn't have time to ask for clarification before the Deacon shouted for me to drive the cart forward. Already the mendicants were pulling on the rope, bringing the end of the style back down to the ground and hoisting the weighted end high into the air.

The sailcloth sling was once more laid ready for filling, and under Jaysen's direction, I emptied the cart into it.

I had barely got the cart moving again before I heard the Deacon shout, "Everybody out."

The sling was whipped away and the third cart was being beckoned forward. The Deacon shouted, "Tallis, get yourself down to the Office of the Combined Hierophants of Aea. See what's going on."
I abandoned the cart to the nearest mendicant. As she and the horse eyed each other uncertainly, I made my way through the streets. Jaysen and Eddna joined me. Even as we got close I could tell something was amiss. I initially thought the smell was emanating from Jaysen, but it was soon obvious that it wasn't just him.
It is difficult to convey in mere words the effect.

<blockquote>
Ordure
Spread thin over walls
Like too little butter
Seeping through windows
Like rain through a shutter
Dripping through shattered roofs
Overflowing the gutter
Complete disorder
</blockquote>

It wasn't easy to tell in the dark but I would have said that the terrace containing the office had taken the worst of the impact. Indeed it looked as if the roof itself had been damaged. Jaysen went off to find somebody who would be interested in paying him to organise the clean-up. Eddna, in full prophet mode, proceeded to lambast the bystanders in the street, verbally flaying her audience, pointing out that the wrath of Aea was not to be casually ignored. I mingled with those going into the office to see what damage had been done.
All the upstairs windows on the side looking towards Exegesis Square had come in, along with a lot of filth. The roof had indeed buckled and the upstairs space was in total disarray.
I merely gazed from the door of the upper room. I confess to being somewhat awestruck at the mess of filth and roof tiles.

It had to be admitted that wherever the Combined Hierophants held their meeting, it wasn't going to be in this building.

Somewhat overwhelmed by what we'd done, thoughtfully I made my way back to the shrine.

📖📖📖

As far as I know, nobody ever formally blamed us. I suspect some of this was planning and some of it was that we were lucky. By the time I arrived back at Exegesis Square the style had been re-erected, the stylite was back in residence and there was even the extra screen to spare the blushes of respectable ladies. Then for the next three days, it rained. Great waves of rain rolled in from the sea, the remnants of storms somewhere far to our west. Whilst it reduced the amount Jaysen could charge the Combined Office for cleaning, the deluge left Exegesis Square so clean it positively sparkled. Indeed even the old sailcloth sling, hung discreetly out at the back of the shrine, washed clean. By the time the sun finally came out, the whole area was immaculate.

At a human level, I came to the conclusion that the inhabitants of the square had, over the years, come to regard us as 'their' shrine. Even if they never darkened the door. So in what they obviously regarded as a theological dispute beyond their understanding, they instinctively supported us. The modesty screen at the top of the style obviously convinced people we were trying to be helpful. Not only that, but on the fourth day, Maljie and the Incumbent returned.

Now the shrine was so tidy that it would have passed inspection by even the most particular archimandrite. The mendicants were on their best behaviour, all of them washed and scrubbed with their robes clean and with hair combed and, where appropriate, beards trimmed. Frankly it would have made me suspicious. Maljie wasn't fooled for a moment.

"So what have you lot been up to."

Innocently, Laxey said, "As instructed, we delayed the formal conclave."

"People are asking questions about just how the contents of somebody's dunny cart came to be dropped on the roof of the Combined Office. They have even questioned Jaysen."

Rather anxiously, the Deacon asked, "What did Jaysen say?"

"He just muttered something about 'bluidy children stealing anything that wasn't tied down.'"

Between ourselves I can almost hear him saying it. Laxey decided to put up some sort of defence. "Apparently they are blaming the order of Aea Unreformed, given that Eddna turned up at the scene of the damage and proceeded to give the credit for it to Aea."

Maljie turned on him. "Given that the order of Aea Unreformed has absolutely no funds, no capital assets, and Eddna is their only stipendiary clerk in holy orders, they're not worth blaming."

"It's true," the Deacon commented, "When you're totally penniless, you have enormous freedom."

"I don't want to experience this freedom!" Maljie's tone was definite.

I decided it might be time to change the subject. "What about the meeting, do you know when it is to be held?"

"Yes, they've borrowed the Council of Sinecurists main chamber. The meeting will be the day after tomorrow."

"So with regard to our incumbent, Tiffy and I got the resignation letter changed. It will no longer stand any sort of scrutiny."

"Good." Maljie sounded somewhat mollified by this. The Deacon asked, "She didn't want to resign did she?"

Maljie said, "I quite forgot to ask her. Never mind, she'd be wasted anywhere but here."

Laxey asked, "And what about the new contender for the post of Autocephalous Patriarch?"

"Hegumen Sydna?" Maljie sounded less sure of herself. "Initially I was in favour of Telbat Spurt keeping the job, if only because we know his weaknesses and foibles. Not only that but I think he's got a soft spot for our shrine."

Laxey asked, "But surely the main reason for supporting Spurt was that Archhierophant Battass Droom would find Sydna easy to manipulate.

"I'm not sure he would. I've spend nearly a month in his company, and I still don't know him, but I don't think he would be a push-over. Also I think he likes us as well."

None of us had heard Maljie so indecisive before. "So do we sit this one out?" The Deacon asked.

"I'm tempted to say yes." Maljie admitted.

With that our impromptu meeting broke up. But as we made our way out into the street, Laxey muttered to me that he wasn't sure what worried him most, the thought that we'd be blamed for the damage to the combined office, or Maljie coming over all thoughtful and uncertain.

📖📖📖

As it was, we were rather thrust into the midst of the proceedings. As the nearest shrine to the Council of Sinecurists building, we were the obvious place to turn to for assistance. Somebody somewhere assumed our mendicants were novices or lay-brethren and had marked us down to supply people to marshal visitors and guide people to their seats. Maljie moved fast. We had managed to get the mendicants properly scrubbed up and presentable for her return, and she immediately held an inspection. A score who couldn't be made presentable, tended to mutter obscenities all the time, or were just hardened recidivists, were packed off to the Fane of the Wise Maiden Halina.

They owed us enough favours and would probably glad of the working party. Laxey, his eye on what the future would probably hold, volunteered to lead them, but Maljie pointed out that as a sub-hierodeacon he was an ordained (after a fashion) member of our staff and thus was expected to be present at the conclave. Then she quick-marched the remaining mendicants, in column of twos, up the Sinecurists' Bridge to the council building. There she met Tiffy who was standing brightly by the main door, directing various people in various directions. After some discussion it was decided that our least literate would form a corridor through the entrance chamber. Anybody who said they were there for the conclave would walk between two widely spaced ranks of mendicants. Those with other business would be allowed to wander untrammelled.

The literate ones were allowed to wander the council chamber, reading the names that staff from the Combined Office were placing on the various boxes. This meant that they would be able to guide people to their seats. Even our shrine had a box, set at the front because we were in theory at least, the hosts. At least our incumbent would get a good view.

In the centre, where there was normally the Secretary's desk and the rostrum for the speaker, this area had been cleared of its usual impedimenta and a large round table had been placed in the middle. It had seats for sixteen archhierophants and hierophants with a special, somewhat larger chair, for the Patriarch. Laxey was given the job of ushering the senior clergy into the chamber and making sure they sat at the right chair.

Whilst there was still space at the back, no provision had been made for lay involvement. This is in itself entirely understandable. What reasonable person wishes to spend a full day or more listening to the bureaucratic workings of a religious organisation? Indeed the sort of person who might wish to do this is probably the sort of person who should be barred for their own good if not ours.

Still, there were teething problems. On overhearing one mendicant, when asked her name, introduce herself as 'Dog Breath', Maljie had to hastily give all of them new names. Thus our female mendicants would introduce themselves as 'Sister' and this was followed by a name from Maljie's approved list. Thus Dog Breath was now to be known as 'Sister Pudicia.' The male mendicants underwent a similar renaming process. In the long run, the discovery that we were apparently a monastic institution with both male and female novices mingling 'promiscuously' meant we gained a somewhat louche reputation. Certainly in the months that followed, we got an increase in potential novices who seemed disappointed when we explained we didn't have a noviciate, just mendicants.

Looking on the bright side, at least we had nothing to do with the catering arrangements. The council building had its own staff and facilities and would handle that side of things. I must admit to being quite relieved when one of the staff came to us and apologised. This lady explained that their dining room couldn't seat all those attending and our mendicants. Would we object to our mendicants dining (at the same time and with the same buffet selection) in a lesser dining room? Personally I could have hugged her. Whilst Maljie had taken great pains over the years to instil basic table manners into the mendicants, it was always an uphill struggle. Too many of them had been too hungry, too often. I had seen the menu that they were going to be presented with. I predicted there would be a short period of stunned disbelief then a mad scramble which would inevitable degenerate into a riot with people being trampled underfoot. At least on our own we could police them. Maljie and Laxey planned to position themselves by the buffet table. Both would carry long temple warden wands.

The great day started well. Our mendicants, roused early, given a good breakfast and then scrubbed under supervision, almost sparkled as they paraded up to the Council Chamber. As they marched each would shout out their new name to Maljie as they passed her. Once at the building they all took up their places and worked well. People arrived, were shown their seats and the hall soon filled.

The last person into the chamber was the Autocephalous Patriarch, Telbat Spurt. In a portentous voice that carried round the chamber, he ordered the doors to be closed so no others could enter. This was the formal start of the meeting. I must confess here that I had never seen Telbat Spurt in action. He was impressive. After leading a brief opening worship, where he delivered a very short, but interesting homily, he walked us through the Declarations of Interest. I suppose it shows my ignorance but I was surprised by the way this section went. Whilst there were sixteen miscellaneous hierophants, some of them held the votes of colleagues living in distant parts who couldn't travel for the meeting. The letters appointing somebody to vote for them by proxy were briefly scrutinised and then the meeting moved on. The patriarch then presented the minutes of the previous meeting and then took us through the action points and matters arising. Here he showed himself to be on top of the subject.

He was either very well briefed or he genuinely did know the minutiae of the issues discussed. Finally the meeting moved to 'petitions.' In this section clergy could raise issues which they felt showed the system was failing. Thus a monk from a distant mountain shrine raised the issue of penance. Apparently the penitentials used by his monastery were so old they were virtually illegible. Not only that but there were three volumes in the set but there were various references to a further two volumes, so they feared that they had lost them.

Hence, at the moment any penance was handed out by the Prior, who based his judgement on what he thought he remembered that the penitential had said. The monastery had sent the monk to petition that the monastery be allowed to adopt a new, and ideally slimmer, penitential and was there one that could be recommended.

The Patriarch dealt with this in two halves. Firstly he asked the assembled conclave whether they were happy for a monastery to dispose of the old penitentials and acquire a new document. This needed agreement because many monasteries had their penitential defined when they were founded. After some discussion round the table there was unanimous agreement that this should be allowed. Then the Patriarch put the more difficult question, which penitential should be used. The discussion, whilst not heated, was certainly conducted by people absolutely confident that the document their institution used was the best that could be suggested. Even as I watched the debate I could see that there were two schools. One felt that any penitential with fewer than five volumes was somehow pandering to unspecified weakness. The other school felt that everything that needed to be said could be said in one slim volume.

Telbat Spurt chaired the meeting beautifully, adding nothing of his own but drawing out all the speakers, and even asking the quieter ones for their contribution. Then, when he felt everybody had said their piece, he suggested that a small committee should be drawn up to look at the various documents, draw together what was best in all of them, and produce something handy. That way, whilst people could of course use the one they had, should anybody need to change, there was something there for them to look at. This was agreed, and the Patriarch offered the petitioning monk a slim penitential used by one of his own institutions.

He pointed out that whilst doubtless deficient in many ways, it was short, easy to read and would be something they could use whilst a more substantive document was being prepared.

Personally I suspected the substantive document would not necessarily appear in this century, would be shunned in the next century, but in three centuries time would be cherished and considered definitive.

The next issue to be raised was the case of our incumbent and the forged letter of resignation. As the incumbent came forward, Tiffy also approached holding the forged letter. Telbat Spurt raised a hand. "Ladies, if I could stop you there. He gestured to the great clock on the wall. "I have tried the patience of those assembled for long enough, if I don't allow them to break for refreshment, I fear for their health." He beckoned our incumbent. "You can at least explain things to me, whilst your assistant can go and provide succour to that monstrous hound of hers who is apparently quietly terrorising the doormen." He turned once more to the assembled multitude. "Right, apparently they are serving a wide selection of infusions in the side room. Other facilities are available through that room, the staff will doubtless direct you."

Thus dismissed, Tiffy gave a nervous little bow and still holding her papers made her way towards the door. By now everybody was on their feet and she was rather swimming against the tide. Ahead of me in the press of people I noticed Battass Droom mutter something to a pair of rather burly servers who were sitting behind him. I was one of the few men not wearing robes, and people tended to assume I was one of the staff employed by the Council Chamber. Thus people tended to ignore me, or even step aside to let me through, assuming I was in some way working. I managed to get closer to Droom and his two servers. I was close enough to hear him say, 'Just get the papers and scare her away.'

With that the two servers left him and started to follow Tiffy. I looked round and fortunately I managed to catch Maljie's eye and gestured towards Tiffy and to the two robed figures closing in on her. Maljie left her place in the queue and followed after me, collecting mendicants as she did so.

Looking at the crowd, I decided to cut right and leave via another door, thus I could go round the corridor on the outside of the chamber. I could now move much faster and was in the corridor before Tiffy. As I made my way towards the door Tiffy would use, I passed the main door out towards the entrance hall. There, standing on his hind legs, looking through the window in the upper part of the door, was her dog. At that point Tiffy entered the corridor, followed very rapidly by the two robed servers. One grabbed her roughly by the shoulder. I did not hesitate, I opened the door and Tiffy's dog, Spot, hurtled past me. He hit Tiffy's attacker full in the chest, knocking him backwards. Tiffy turned round and kicked the second man under the chin as he sidestepped the melee on the floor and tried to grab Tiffy. As I reached her, the second man sprawled unconscious on the ground, Tiffy turned to me and said, inconsequentially, "Mother always insisted I learn to dance."

I suspected I knew her dancing instructor.

Maljie and a number of mendicants came through the door. Without anybody saying anything, the two men were gagged and trussed up. Maljie gestured to a side door, "Down there, get a hand cart."

One of the mendicant asked, "A sea-faring life?"

"Yes."

The two men disappeared. I asked, "A sea-faring life? Are you selling them to the crimp?"

"I let the mendicants do it when we need to dispose of people like that. I think of the money as a nice little bonus for them."

I thought about this, "Does this happen often?"

"Not as often as it should." Maljie looked at Tiffy. "I

think you and I should go and get a coffee. You still have the papers?"

"Yes they never got close to them."

The two women, Spot following at heel, went back into the chamber. I'm not sure which of the three was swaggering the most.

Chapter 12

The Patriarch called the meeting to order, and both the incumbent and Tiffy once more took their places. The incumbent clearly stated her complaint. Somebody had forged a letter of resignation for her. This caused a stir. I overheard one senior cleric whisper to his neighbour that this was unprecedented. He remembered somebody feeding an unwanted incumbent to the gorlix, but never forging a resignation. What, he mused, was the world coming to? Our incumbent then asked Tiffy to show each of the conclave around the table the forgery and a genuine specimen of her writing. Tiffy started with the Patriarch and slowly went round the table giving each archhierophant time to make up his mind as to whether it was a forgery. I watched Battass Droom as closely as I could when Tiffy showed him the forgery. I was intrigued to know whether he realised that the forgery wasn't the forgery we assumed had been his. He made no reaction, merely passing the papers back to Tiffy and she continued to work her way around the circle.

As Tiffy arrived back at the Patriarch he looked around the circle of his peers. "Well?"

One said, "A forgery, obviously."

There were nods of agreement from around the table. Telbat Spurt appeared to study the documents again then said, "Battass, you have a connection with the staircase shrine. You are the obvious person to investigate the forgery.

Given the agreement of the conclave I will appoint

you as my personal representative to investigate.
That way you will have the full authority of the
Patriarch at your disposal, people will answer to you
as they would answer to me." He looked around the
conclave. Each of the assembled hierophants gave
their agreement. Battass Droom also agreed but
managed to look as if he was suffering from severe
stomach cramps as he did so.

The Patriarch turned to the incumbent. "You are
confirmed in your position, the letter is an obvious
forgery, and archhierophant Droom will investigate it
immediately."

Then as if it had just occurred to him, "I say Battass,
a report on my desk in a fortnight."

With that he leaned back in his seat. "And our next
petition please."

📖📖📖

As the next petitioner stepped forward I was torn
between listening to him and watching Maljie and the
incumbent who appeared to be deep in conversation.
The choice of Battas Droom to investigate what was
probably his own misdemeanour was somewhat
eccentric, to say the least.

I gave up trying to out-think the Patriarch and turned
my attention to the petitioner. This was a decision I
came to regret. Over the years I have dozed lightly
through many tedious presentations. Indeed I have
long been blessed with the gift of coming gently
awake with as little fuss as when I fell gently into
slumber. You will not see Tallis Steelyard start guiltily
awake wondering what he's missed. But the third
petitioner was a master of dreariness. Looking around
I could see heads nodding and eyes drooping.

Certainly the case was remarkably complicated. The
'Shrine of Aea Aspirant' claimed that the 'Fane of Aea
on Sneaves Lane' was under their jurisdiction and had
not been paying the agreed contribution.

We were being treated to a point by point review of every aspect of the dispute which seemed to stretch back before the beginning of time. I too was starting to nod.

Then the Patriarch's voice cut through the fog that was beginning to descend on my. "You, Sir, are a lawyer."

I snapped awake and looked at the petitioner. He wore the robes of a lay brother. He responded, "Patriarch, I am an advocate and have confraternity."

"That does not contradict my statement. Where is your incumbent?"

A tall, thin woman stood up from her seat and moved forward. The Patriarch turned the focus of her wrath on her. "Sister Acoemetae, I am at a loss. What in Aea's name do you mean by using a lawyer? Petitioners using legal counsel to advance their petition is prohibited by canon."

The sister rallied. "Patriarch, he is a lay brother."

"Has he taken the three vows?"

"Two only, Patriarch. Obedience and stability. As he still has to support himself, for we are not a wealthy shrine, he has not taken the third vow, conversion of manners."

"So he has taken the vow of obedience. Good." The Patriarch looked round and obviously spotted somebody. "Hegumen Falan, you have once again contrived to grace us with your presence." The Patriarch sounded genuinely pleased to see Falan. An elderly monk stood up. "Patriarch, ours is a small house, quiet, isolated. Thus I try and ensure that as many of us can attend the conclave as possible." He paused briefly, "I realise people might accuse me of an unhealthy craving for excitement, but it does us good to get out."

"It does indeed, Falan. And you shall return one lay brother stronger than you left. Apparently this creature who has been assaulting our ears with his cant is sworn to obedience. So as his superior I have decided he needs to spend a decade with you for the good of his spiritual development."

Hegumen Falan bowed. "It shall be as you command, Patriarch."

The Patriarch turned his gaze to the stunned advocate. "A good day. I have achieved two marvels. I have rid Port Naain of a lawyer, and I have managed to get Hegumen Falan to speak in a meeting of the conclave." He dismissed the advocate with a wave of his hand. "Now I want somebody with sense who knows Port Naain." His eye fell on our incumbent. "Can you have one of your temple wardens investigate the situation and let us know what the in the forty-seven canonical hells is going on."

Our incumbent glanced at Maljie and then across at me. "Certainly."

"Excellent, we'll break for lunch now, and then the afternoon is given over to meditation and spiritual exercises. If you can pick your investigator over lunch, then they'll doubtless be back here to explain the situation by the time we gather in the late afternoon for the next formal part of our meeting."

📖📖📖

So I had a busy afternoon ahead of me. It was obvious that I was the expendable one, and perhaps our incumbent had the hope that I would merely report what I found. Maljie is a little prone to report, brusquely, on the steps she took to rectify the problem she found.

I first went to the Shrine of Aea Aspirant. It's on the edge of the Commercial Quarter and I could visit it on my way to the other shrine. I had been there before, it is a new building with pretensions. Imagine, if you would, that you had a plot of land rather larger than you needed for a house. You then asked a friend of yours who built barns to build you a barn on the site. Not an especially large barn, but a barn built properly using decent brick and new timber.

Then a little embarrassed by the fact you only had a barn, you asked another friend who had read too many fifty-dreg romances set in Partann to ornament it. So across the front the barn there suddenly sprouted a cacophony of turrets, cupolas, spires and even a tower. Inside a third friend had obviously run amok with stucco. Then finally, those bare areas not rendered grossly over-ornate with stucco were painted with frescos. The seating was composed of simple bench seats, painted in primary colours. It looked as if somebody had wondered whether it was possible to drive out bad taste with sheer excess. Looking at the result the various artists had achieved, I would have been tempted to say that the answer was definitely no.

There was a temple warden apparently on duty, but it wasn't until I showed him my warrant signed by the Patriarch that he deigned to notice me. He seemed sunk in his own private world of misery. I explained my purpose and he grunted sadly and led me to a small room that had been added to the back of the barn. It was obviously something of an afterthought, the original designer never having realised the need for office space.

The temple-warden silently opened an account book and gestured to it. Now my apprenticeship to Miser Mumster was served some years ago, but I still have the knack that few other poets have. I can look at a set of accounts and understand them. These accounts showed a sorry tale. The costs of building the shrine had not merely soaked up the money set aside for the purpose, the incumbent at the time had borrowed more money to finish the works. Since then the shrine had fought a desperate losing battle to pay off the debt. Indeed in recent years they had abandoned debt repayment for the slightly less fanciful task of merely keeping up with the interest payments.

Even with the irregular contribution from the Fane of Aea on Sneaves Lane matters were obviously spiralling out of control.

I closed the book and passed it back to him. There was nothing to say.

Next I found myself walking briskly through the Sump looking for the Fane of Aea on Sneaves Lane. The shrine wasn't difficult to find. Many years ago somebody had turned the front room of a house into a shrine. As far as I could tell, this involved putting an extra door in so you could reach the shrine without going through the other two downstairs rooms. Thus the house had two front doors. One was marked, 'Granan Velon, Cobbler.' The other stood open and led to the shrine. The shrine itself had one painting of Aea as an elderly lady being helped by small children as she struggled home with her shopping. There was a lectern for the preacher to put their notes on, a dozen hard wooden chairs for the congregation (each chair was different), a mop bucket and mop for the temple warden and a fireplace. Given it was summer I didn't expect to see it lit, but I was surprised to find a lady down on her knees polishing it with a black lead polish.

She saw me arrive and stood up. "Hello, I'm Thekla Velon, the temple warden."

"I was asked to find out what the problem is between your shrine and the Shrine of Aea Aspirant."

"It's simple, they want money, and we haven't got any."

"But why have they claimed that you ought to pay them money in the first place?"

"It's a bit complicated..." She sounded hesitant.

"I'm a poet, try me with a simplified version first."

"The house was owned by the Patriarch's estate. When they were building the Shrine of Aea Aspirant, and they needed to borrow, the Patriarch of the day gifted us to them. Both to use as security and also to pay rent."

"So they are entitled to rent."

"Rent for a cobbler's shop. They also want rent for the shrine and the amount they're asking you'd think we were a major fane with dancing girls and thousands visiting during a major festival."

She showed me their rent book and the paperwork. I was thinking hard as I walked back to the Council Chamber and the Conclave. On my arrival I asked to see the Patriarch, and was shown into the small private room he had had put aside for him. He greeted me with white wine and listened in silence as I explained the problem.

"Have you a solution for me as well, Master Steelyard."

"Given that a Patriarch is at the root of the problem, it struck me a Patriarch could solve the problem."

"And how much is it going to cost me?"

His shrewdness was unnerving. "I suggest you buy the house and shrine in Sneaves Lane back. For enough to clear the debts of Aea Aspirant. Then they should be viable. Then you charge the Sneaves Lane Shrine rent for the cobbler's shop and nothing for the shrine."

He pondered my advice. I added, "So on the books, you've not lost money, you've merely made a wise, long term capital investment."

"I was told you were a poet, Master Steelyard, indeed I've attended affairs where you performed."

"I served my time with a usurer."

"Then I shall take the advice of a usurer, seeing as how it is being proffered free." At this point a minor cleric of one of the lesser orders poked his head around the door, "They are assembling in the Council Chamber."

The Patriarch stood up. "I suggest you make your own way into the chamber, I'm not sure you'd want to be too closely associated with me." He paused, "But before you go, can you recommend a forensic accountant?"

"Well there are always Mesdames Marisol and Chesini Clogchipper."

"Excellent. I'll get in touch with them as soon as I have time."

I took my seat. I'd chosen a place near the front but at the 'wrong side' of the dais. This allowed me to see the conclave gathered around the table, but it also meant I got a good view of most of the audience. Frankly over the years I've always found the audience far more interesting that those who strut upon the stage mangling their lines and painfully masticating the cadence of the words. So I was able to watch people filing in and taking their place. I noted that this time, Tiffy sat with Maljie and Spot, taking the seats behind our Incumbent. Finally the Patriarch entered. He came in from the back of the hall, walking down to the dais at the front. He leaned on his staff of office, an old man walking alone. It struck me that Telbat Spurt was a fine actor, and that the role of Patriarch was one of his finest. As he moved down, people would stand up in respect for his office, sitting down as he passed, a wave passing through the auditorium. I would hire him to preside over an evening's entertainment, but I suspect he would steal the show.

Before he took his chair he turned and bowed to the others in the conclave, and then he turned and bowed to those of us sitting around. Finally he spoke.

"I have had a report about the situation as it pertains to the Shrine of Aea Aspirant and the Fane of Aea on Sneaves Lane."

The hall was now silent, I suspect everybody was wondering just what he was going to do.

"The Patriarch will purchase the Sneaves Lane site from the Shrine of Aea Aspirant. This will clear their debts." He turned and looked to a stunned Sister Acoemetae. Sternly he said, "I will leave the good sister to decide whether this is proof that I am gracious enough to overlook her use of a lawyer," and here you could hear the laughter in his voice, "Or whether it is my thanks for her allowing me the pleasure of banishing a lawyer into the outer darkness."

Hegumen Falan stood up, "When you talk about 'outer darkness', does this mean you have seen my request for more lamp oil? In the north the normal allocation goes nowhere."

"Relax Falan, the allocation for your monastery is tripled. You shall indeed be a light in the darkness, literally as well as spiritually."

He paused as if finding his place in an unwritten script. "And the Sneaves Lane Fane. This shall continue before, but will pay the normal rent owing from the cobbler's shop, but will pay no rent from the fane itself. I would be embarrassed if, when in due course I must appear before Aea, that the first thing I have to do is to sign her rent book!"

With this he sat down and there was a ripple of spontaneous applause. Then he said, "I believe Archhierophant Battass Droom has a motion to raise."

Droom rose to his feet. "Yes, it is my sad duty to proclaim that the Patriarch is a disgrace, is unfit to hold office and I propose that Hegumen Sydna, a most saintly man, be elected to the post. I have here," and here he raised a wad of papers, "Twenty-three proxy votes from those who cannot be present but are entitled to vote. They all feel that this disgraceful state of affairs cannot be allowed to continue."

He passed the wad of papers to the Patriarch and then proceeded to examine, in some detail, various of the charges against the Patriarch. It was then that I realised why Telbat Spurt had entered as he did. When he had acted and spoken, he had done so with a certain majesty, a greatness which he shared with his audience. Droom spoke well enough yet seemed as if he lacked confidence, as if he feared he'd missed something that might trip him up.

Indeed Spurt's performance left Droom looking like a petty bureaucrat who was pestering somebody over various minor infringements.

The Patriarch sat and listened without emotion, until

Droom seemed to gain confidence, and at this point Telbat Spurt rose. "A point of order." He turned to the two clerks who were off to one side taking notes of the meeting. "Lady and gentleman, did not I just this morning appoint Battass Droom as my personal representative with the full authority of the Patriarch at his disposal?"

The clerks went through the motions of looking through their notes. Then the lady said, "Yes, Patriarch you did."

"And under the canons of our order, is not one thus appointed ineligible to raise motions or vote at a conclave, for as long as the appointment lasts." His tone changed, becoming more didactic as he addressed the audience. "This was instituted many years ago. It ensures that the Patriarch cannot elevate people who are then beholden to him, merely to harvest their votes."

As she flicked through a thick volume, the secretary said, "It is indeed so. Also, if I remember correctly….." The council chamber was silent as everybody watched her find the section she was looking for.

"Ah here it is. Fourteen, subsections one, two, and three. 'A person so appointed may not vote, solicit and cast proxy votes, nor may they attempt to convince others to vote or not to vote.' And subsection two says, 'A person so appointed may not raise motions, neither may they speak for or against motions.'"

In tones of casual interest, Telbat Spurt asked, "And what does subsection three say?" Even as he said it, I thought, 'he knows, he's read it.'

The secretary, in a clear voice, read, "A person so appointed should not attend conclave meetings, save at the express invitation of Patriarch. This invitation must be issued in writing a week before the conclave, and should any member of the conclave formally disapprove, the invitation must be withdrawn."

The Patriarch turned to Battass Droom. "To spare the blushes of the conclave, I do not issue any invitation, thus I am afraid Battass Droom must leave this conclave." Then with every sign of magnanimity he added, "But obviously he may watch the proceedings from one of the seats that surround us."

Silently, Droom stood up, pushing his chair back, and walked out of the council chamber.

Even before he had left the chamber, the Patriarch said calmly. "Still, whilst it was handled extremely badly, Hegumen Sydna has been proposed as Patriarch. I would not wish it to be thought that I wished to thwart the wishes of this conclave on a mere technicality. I therefore nominate him. Battass Droom has elicited my vices. All I can say is I am thankful he didn't know me better, or his list would have been longer and more detailed. Of Hegumen Sydna I have heard nothing bad. Indeed over the years that I have known him, I have always relied on his spiritual wisdom. He is perhaps one of the best among us. Now I am going to sit down and let our conclave vote. Each of the members around the table will write on their slate the number of votes they are authorised to cast and who they're casting them for."

Each of the fifteen remaining picked up the piece of chalk by his slate and after some thought they started writing. When the last one had finished, the Patriarch gestured to the two clerks, and each went round the table, tallying the votes separately. They then compared totals. After a brief pause, they went round again, checking. Finally the lady came and stood before the Patriarch.

"We find fifteen votes cast for Hegumen Sydna and fifteen votes cast for Telbat Spurt. We await your casting vote to decide the issue."

Telbat Spurt stood up and looked over the conclave to the audience beyond. "I will not cast my vote. I ask Hegumen Sydna to join me here, and between us, if everybody is willing, we will decide on who will be your next patriarch."

He looked at the conclave gathered around the table. "Is this agreed?"

I saw the senior clergy exchanging puzzled glances. This was unprecedented, and they were not sure of the implications. Eventually one of them said, "I agree."

Around the table, there was a ripple of agreement as each, relieved of the responsibility of being first, fell into line.

Then Telbat Spurt looked over the conclave to the audience in general. With a sweep of his arms which included them all he asked, "Is this agreed."

Slowly, but with gathering momentum, people started shouting 'yes'. I noticed that our mendicants, swept up in the occasion, had joined the shout.

He waited for Sydna to join him at the top table and then turned back to the audience. "Given we have two patriarchs and one official residence in the city, it is not fitting for us to return there. After all, who is host and who is guest? I suggest that we both retire to the nearest shrine whilst we discuss these matters and bring things to a resolution. So we must now impose upon the incumbent of the Shrine of Aea in her Aspect as the Personification of Tempered Enthusiasm."

I thought our incumbent was going to faint.

Chapter 13

Next morning I received a note asking me to present myself at the shrine later that morning. I arrived and drifted into the ostiary's cell by the door. The Deacon was holding a rather crowded open house as he welcomed the usual suspects. Maljie, Laxey and the Prophet Weldun were already there. I'd barely taken a seat before a mendicant stuck their head round the door and said, "The incumbent wants you all in the library."

This surprised me. The last time I had been in the

library, admittedly some months ago, it was a dark gloomy hole. There was one, small, window, which cast a little light on the grimy stone walls. Around the walls there were shelves of slate flags, on which reposed, in picturesque disorder, a lot of books of uncertain vintage. The one battered table was piled high with tomes, most open, relinquished as the person searching for something had either found what they needed, or abandoned the search as fruitless. I was in for a shock. The deacon opened the door with the air of a conjurer producing a particularly clever trick. The library had indeed changed. The slate shelves had gone. The walls had all been beautifully clad in a light coloured wood. They were lined with wooden shelves and the ceiling had been painted white. Judging by the way light streamed in through the window, I first thought it had been enlarged. Closer examination showed that it had merely been cleaned. All the books were carefully placed on the shelves, and there were two tables, one for the repair of books, the other for scholarship.

Our incumbent watched as the Patriarch and Hegumen Sydna were browsing the shelves.

The Patriarch reached for a book, "Look, they've even got a copy of Bartlet's 'Anthropopathism, Hypothetical Universalism, and their place in Postsuppositional apologetics.'"

Hegumen Sydna looked at him, "Isn't that heretical?"

The Patriarch shrugged, "It could be two centuries since anybody read Bartlet anyway. I doubt if anybody can remember."

They obviously noticed that we had arrived. The Patriarch looked at the Hegumen, "Should I tell them, or will you?"

Hegumen Sydna smiled. "You tell them, I want to watch their reaction."

"Well firstly, because either both of us, or neither of us, is patriarch, we have decided that you should just address us as Telbat or Sydna.

Secondly, neither of us actually wants to be patriarch. I don't want the job because I've done it. Synda here knows he doesn't want it without even trying it, because he's a lot wiser than I am. He wishes to return to his monastery and I am going to go into semi-retirement. I am to be incumbent of the shrine at Tideholt." Telbat's tone grew almost nostalgic. "Warm winters, pleasant summers, beaches, fine wine, decent fishing and a small but loyal populace who don't bother you with theology." He pulled himself together, "Thirdly, we have been given the authority to pick a Patriarch, and we have given it a lot of thought. Bearing in mind our experiences over the years, we have decided to make Maljie, Patriarch."

Behind me there was a crash. The incumbent had fainted, Laxey, in trying to catch her, had bounced off Maljie who stood stunned.

"But I cannot be a Patriarch, I'm a woman."

Telbat smiled at her, "In the last three hundred years we have had over a dozen female patriarchs. They all abjured the title of Matriarch."

"But I'm not ordained."

Sydna waved a dismissive hand, "You are in the presence of not one but two patriarchs. Not only can we ordain you, we could make a fair stab at having you declared a living saint."

The incumbent, who had recovered consciousness, whimpered a little at that.

"But I don't want the bluidy job."

"Perfect. Anybody who wants the job is almost by definition unsuited to it."

"But I'm not going to do it."

"Then find us somebody who will do it."

Maljie wagged a finger under Telbat's nose. "You conniving bastard, you've set me up to do your dirty business."

Sydna said, apologetically, "Well I did suggest you as well."

Maljie rounded on him, "After all I've done for you!"

"I know, the lichen smuggling was most expertly done."

At this point a mendicant appeared at the door, the Deacon had sent her to get the brandy. Laxey took the bottle glanced at Maljie and the incumbent, took a long pull from the bottle and handed it to me. I drank some and passed the bottle down to the incumbent. I felt that if Maljie was given a bottle, in her current state she was more likely to belabour somebody with it than drink from it.

Prophet Weldun, as the unlikely voice of reason, said, "So we have to find a Patriarch. Basically the prime qualification for the job is that they are ordained and don't want the job."

"Well we can always arrange an ordination, so perhaps we could say, 'Worthy of ordination.'"

Telbat looked thoughtful, "How about, 'can be ordained without offending decency too much.' I can think of plenty of people who have been ordained in the past whom I wouldn't describe as 'worthy'."

Our Prophet persevered, "So in reality, we're going to have to find somebody we can pressure into taking the job."

Sydna said, "But don't worry too much. After all, Maljie is the perfect candidate."

Our incumbent was cuddling the bottle and singing quietly to it.

Laxey asked, "So setting Maljie aside for the moment, have you a list of other preferred candidates. One of the archhierophants for example?"

Telbat said, "Not the archhierophants. No archhierophant has ever been suited for the job of Patriarch. Their role is far too tied up in administration and they lack the imagination or drive necessary."

Sydna said, "But yes, we have a couple of other suggestions."

I produced an indelible pencil and a scrap of paper. "Could we have the suggestions then?"

Telbat said, "Well the best choice would be Brother Tanai, he's currently preaching in the Chatterfield area of Partann."

Sydna said, "Telbat." There was a warning note in his voice.

"Well actually he seems to have fallen out with a number of the local lordlings and we've not heard from him for a month or so."

"Telbat."

"Well you tell them then!"

Sydna said, "He is incarcerated in the dungeon of Blackthorn Tower, about ten miles from Chatterfield. He has probably not been executed or tortured to death, yet."

I noted this down, and asked, "And the next?"

"Sister Alanette."

Laxey asked, "And where do we have to rescue her from?"

Sydna said, "She is in Port Naain, she's connected with the Temple of Aea in her Aspect as the Personification of Chastity."

I said, "My cousin Thela is a temple dancer there, she'll probably know her."

Prophet Weldun asked, "Your cousin is still a temple dancer, but she's older even than you."

I confess I snapped at him, "She can still out-dance women half her age."

Sydna said, "And our third possible choice is..." He paused as I took up the pencil again, "Hegumen Falan, you might have met him in the conclave."

Laxey said, "That's handy, he's in town."

"Alas no, he discovered a boat was sailing late yesterday. His plan is to take the boat to Sweethaven and then march inland from there."

Telbat added, "But you needn't worry about him. We are sending Battass Droom to him."

I asked, "An interesting choice if you don't mind me saying."

"Well it will keep him out of Port Naain, limit his plotting, and he'll be away for up to a month anyway.

That will give our forensic accountants Marisol and Chesini Clogchipper time to go through his books."

"Won't he just get the next boat up?"

"Oh we won't tell him Falan got the boat. We'll send him off overland desperately trying to catch up."

Prophet Weldun asked, "But what if he asks Falan and Falan accepts, and at the same time we've asked somebody and they accept?"

"Don't worry." Sydna spoke before Telbat could answer, "Falan is old enough and wise enough not to want the job and Battass Droom doesn't want him to have it anyway."

"But," Telbat added, "Falan would make a damned good Patriarch."

Sydna brought the interview to a close, "Still, you've got a lot to think about, don't let us detain you. Oh and Tallis, could you go round to see the Clogchippers, you'll have to arrange entry into Battass Droom's humble abode."

Abandoning the incumbent and the brandy bottle, we fled back to the ostiary's cell by the door

📖📖📖

We sat in silence for a while. The Deacon had made coffee. I felt that if I made some suggestions as to how we would proceed I could at least help steer the planning.

"Because I've got a good indirect contact with Sister Alanette, why don't I tackle her, whilst a couple of you go down into Partann to find this Brother Tanai?"

There was silence once more, which I felt wasn't a good sign. Then Prophet Weldun said, "Well you cannot expect me to go trailing down to Partann at my age."

Laxey added, "And I'll have to stay here to continue with my duties and to support the incumbent. After all she's got two patriarchs disporting themselves in her shrine."

I had to fight my corner here. "I cannot go, I've got work to do, Patrons who will want me organising events."

Maljie signed. "Laxey can support the incumbent, Weldun can find out more about Sister Alanette, Tallis and I will go down to Partann to find this Brother Tanai."

"But what about my patrons?"

"It's summer, most of them will be out of town and we'll soon deal with the others."

"I've still got to see the Clogchippers, and arrange for them to see Battass Droom's accounts."

"Do you think he'll have any?"

That was a good question but one I'd pondered. Apparently all the archhierophants have them because they're responsible for quite complicated tasks. How detailed his will be I don't know. Given the reputation of the man I could imagine them being detailed to the last dreg. Probably with entries like, 'Resale of confectionery appropriated from small children, 2 dregs.' "Yes and I cannot leave Port Naain until Droom has left and I can get an accountant into his office."

📖📖📖

First we went to see my patrons. Maljie demanded a list of those who I needed to see. Then she accompanied me to see them. I am struggling to find a suitably embarrassing analogy. Imagine having your mother drag you in front of a series of school teachers, explaining that you cannot attend school because of an embarrassing ailment. Admittedly having never really attended school (and having only the vaguest memories of my mother) I can only attempt to imagine this situation, but I hope it helps you visualise my plight.

My clients were informed that the Patriarch and Maljie needed me to plunge into the maelstrom of Uttermost Partann to rescue some poor innocent monk.

I confess that if I had been offered up this scenario, I would have asked why they were sending a poet, rather than a mercenary company. Still not everybody sees things with the clarity of a poet, so none of my patrons put their finger on this obvious weakness in the argument.

There again, some of my patrons were dazzled by the fact that the Patriarch had asked me to do this. An even larger group were overwhelmed by the fact that Maljie had demanded my services. A small and somewhat more select group obviously didn't believe a word of it but were willing to go along with the cover story on the grounds that they would get to hear an excellent tale when I finally arrived home. This done, I was sent back to the barge to pack and explain to Shena, my lady wife, just exactly what I was up to. I was given the next day to arrange matters for the accountants. Maljie muttered something about having a word with some old business partners, and talking to people in the Black Grapes.

I'm assuming that her old business partners were usurers, but I wasn't going to pry. As for the Black Grapes, it is a nice enough inn. The clientele is interesting. A lot of Condottieri drink there when they're in Port Naain. You also get a lot of Partannese who have just delivered messages and are waiting for replies. On top of this you'll get the poseurs who want to be considered as tough enough to be condottieri, along with a smattering of Urlan who drop in looking for old friends. Looking at it dispassionately, I suspect that Maljie would probably know a fair number of the regulars professionally. Still I wasn't entirely convinced, condottieri forces have been known to disappear into Partann and never come back. As she bid me good evening I merely commented, "Frankly, I suspect you'd be better off tying a blade between your toes so we can cut ourselves free when we're tied up ready for disposal by this lordling we're going to negotiate with."

The two sisters, Marisol and Chesini Clogchipper, had put their business together under straitened circumstances, as they tried to discover which of his business competitors had 'disappeared' their father. Their elder brother was a condottieri man-at-arms and surgeon. He was in the habit of sending patients to his mother to recuperate and when you have gallant young men and attractive and intelligent young women, things happen. What happened was that a lot of injured mercenaries finding their careers at a fork in the road, discovered accountancy. Thus throughout the profession it was accepted that accountancy practices were universally staffed by middle aged and older professionals, perpetually hunched from spending too long sitting over innumerable ledgers, squinting at the endless columns of figures though pince-nez. Unless you hired the Clogchippers, in which case your accountant was likely to be a lady accompanied by her 'clerk'. The clerk would normally be tall, broad-shouldered and narrow-waisted, with the ability to carry his own weight in ledgers, to disarm even the most truculent usurer's bully with a cheery grin, a witty aside, or a competently wielded broadsword.

Thus when I was told I would meet Marisol Clogchipper and two clerks to escort them to the abode of Battass Droom, I had some idea what to expect.

The archhierophant lived in a house provided by the order, and his household also consisted of members of the order. Thus matters were easier to arrange than you might suppose. Droom had been seen riding north. Even as he disappeared from sight, his housekeeper had to go to nurse her ailing mother. In reality her ailing mother was a widowed costermonger with whom she had a long established relationship.

The only remaining member of staff was the doorkeeper and odd-job man. He was a friend of a friend of Laxey's. He had been invited out for a couple of drinks, and Laxey assured us that he could guarantee that the few drinks went on into the early hours.

Finally, because the property belonged to the order, the order had a door key. So rather than have to resort to picking the lock, we just let ourselves in like the respectable professionals we were.

The house intrigued me. Throughout the order, the clergy tend to be provided with furnished lodgings. In reality the clergy tend to restrict the order's furniture to the study, dining room, kitchen and servants' rooms. Most will try to gather up enough of their own furniture to furnish their bedroom and drawing room. As far as I could see, Battass Droom had no furniture of his own and just used what the order gave him.

We made a swift inspection of all the rooms, spending longer in the bedroom and study. The bedroom contained a simple single bed of the sort we have for mendicants. A plain timber frame with a mesh of rope to support the mattress. Rather than something stuffed with shredded wool or down, Droom had a simple sawdust stuffed palliasse. Other than that the room was only sparsely furnished, a wardrobe which contained nothing but robes and similar. It appeared that he had no secular clothing.

The study was more interesting. Marisol and her clerks soon found the ledgers. Indeed they found them so rapidly that they grew suspicious and searched again. They discovered two more ledgers hidden in plain sight in the bookshelves, with bindings proclaiming them to be the collective sayings of a dozen minor prophets from a previous century.

I confess to having been rather taken by his library. Many of the books were obviously his rather than the order's. Judging by what was well thumbed, Droom read history for pleasure.

Also there were a lot of three volume novels, but these were rather more elevated than the usual tales. Not for Droom the endless tales of lovers separated by fate, forced to roam the world trying to get back together, facing increasingly improbably ordeals until finally reunited in the final chapter.

Droom preferred something more cerebral, the fall and rise of dynasties, the subtle political interplay of clans who, in a less civilised environment, one might call 'warring'. It was obvious that even in his reading, our archhierophant enjoyed intrigue.

Still, we had spent long enough in his house. Making sure everything was as we left it, taking only the ledgers, we left as unobtrusively as we'd entered. Four days later, having copied out the ledgers, all the while checking for the secret signs and invisible inks, they equally unobtrusively put them back

📖📖📖

Next morning Maljie and I boarded the Elusive. One of the many ships which ply the coasts of Partann, the Elusive was unusual in that it sailed further south than most. In Port Naain it is easy enough to find a ship to take you south as far as Prae Ducis. Indeed it's probably a rare day when you cannot find one. But if you want to go further south, ships are few and far between.

Indeed if you want to go to, for example, Chatterfield, most people would sail to Prae Ducis and pick up a boat south from there. There are quite a lot of boats will provide that service but you rarely see them in Port Naain. After all Port Naain has drowning posts for pirates, hangs in chains those brigands who come ashore from ships to ravage the land and even has a harsh attitude to the minor peccadillos of smugglers. Between ourselves I am certain the Elusive was a smuggler, but just a very competent one that had managed to avoid discovery.

The journey south was quiet enough.

Like most smugglers, the Elusive didn't bother putting in at ports north of Prae Ducis. After all there are plenty of legitimate traders serving those ports. We sailed south to Chatterfield without stopping. Still the trip was not without interest. On one evening when we were not far from Prae Ducis, I decided to take a walk on the deck before retiring to bed. There was a sail to our stern and whilst I cannot say that I stood staring at it, over half an hour, as I glanced in that direction, the sail held its position. So it was sailing in our direction, without lights. On the other hand, it has to be admitted that we were also sailing without lights. Still none of the crew seemed to even notice the ship. This, to me, was not a good sign. Next day I mentioned it to Maljie, and she was dismissive.

"It's just another ship, these things happen."

"And south of Prae Ducis, these things happen because pirates are shadowing their prey."

"Tallis you're a poet and far too imaginative."

"I want to know why none of the watch keepers made any comment about it."

"Perhaps because they'd been paid to keep their mouths shut?"

"Yes, but who by?"

"Me. Now shut up and let me get on with working out what we're going to do when we land."

What we did when we landed was walk ashore in disguise. Maljie once more donned the robes of a stipendiary maiden penitent. I merely dressed in the nondescript habit I had worn in the north. Only this time my footwear was my own and far more suitable for walking. We passed quietly through the small town of Chatterfield. Nobody seemed to take any notice of us, and the town itself seemed quiet. We walked down streets of unpretentious half-timbered houses. What stonework that was visible was composed of a patchwork of beautiful cut stone, as if the stones had been taken from different building projects. Everything seemed well organised, there was a large drain down the middle of each street and the municipality seemed to employ night soil collectors who mucked out the drain at reasonable intervals. We passed two women with shovels and long leather aprons, shovelling ordure out of the drain and into their cart. We passed through the southern gate and Maljie led me along the road heading south. It was pleasant enough countryside. The area around the town was comparatively open. Indeed I did wonder if this was a matter of policy, to ensure that nobody could creep up under cover to make a surprise assault on the gate. Once we'd walked further the area was broken up with small copses and woods. In one clump of trees I could see ruins. How old they were I couldn't say, but I have been told that the locals can find agriculture difficult in places because you are always digging into the remains of forgotten cities. Certainly I could see where the burghers of Chatterfield got their building materials from.

We had walked for perhaps an hour when an old man almost ran out of farm.

"Holy mother, can you come in please. My sister is dying and wants a word with somebody."

Maljie carefully arranged her habit and brushed the dust of the road off it and led me into the house. We walked through a small courtyard. Around the courtyard was a portico built from mismatched pillars, and from the portico you could enter the various rooms of the house. Here in the shade there were perhaps a dozen people sitting, waiting. Nodding to them we were led into a large kitchen. Our guide pointed to a door, "My sister's room is though there."

Maljie opened the door and walked in, closing it firmly behind her. The guide and I were left outside.

"Will she be all right with my sister? I'd hate the Holy Mother to be shocked at anything my sister has to say."

The idea of Maljie being easily shocked was one I'd not come across before. I bowed my head gravely.

"The stipendiary maidens penitent are a small order, but they are wise and the darker areas of the human spirit are well known to them."

I'm not sure that reassured him or frightened him into silence. As it was we sat there for quite some time without speaking. Nobody came into the room and I may even have drifted off. Then the door to the sister's room opened and Maljie stepped out. Her face was drawn and her voice was sorrowful when she spoke. "Your sister has passed on. May Aea receive her."

The old man covered his face with his hands and we waited for him to recover his self-control. "Thank you Holy Mother."

Maljie held up two sealed pieces of paper. "Her will. I must meet the family."

"They are gathered outside."

We went back and I for one blinked as the bright sunlight hit me. The family all looked up nervously. They had a right to be nervous, in many parts of Partann, inheritance is still down the maternal line. Maljie looked round the group. "Could Ballan and Colnie step forward please."

This was not a question, it was a command. A young man and young woman rather uncertainly stood up. I would have said they were between eighteen and twenty.

"Your grandmother said that a serious wrong has been done to you. On her death bed she saw no more reason to prevent the embarrassment of hypocrites. You are not half-brother and half-sister. Indeed even your grandmother wasn't sure who your fathers were, but she was damned sure they weren't your mother's husband. You are free to marry if you wish. There was a sob from the group. A middle-aged women threw her apron over her head, her body wracked with tears, another woman of a similar age put her arm round her to comfort her. An older man stood stunned. The two young people moved instinctively closer together.

Maljie held up two pieces of paper. "There are two wills. One says that if Ballan and Colnie marry today in Chatterfield, they can take the will with them and your grandmother's lawyer will deal with it."

She held out one of the wills, Ballan looked at Colnie. Colnie grabbed the will with one hand and Ballan with the other, and the young couple ran towards Chatterfield.

Maljie held up the second will. "I will now burn this. If the young people weren't allowed to marry, her entire estate was to be left to the Shrine of Aea in Her Aspect as the Personification of Chastity in Chatterfield."

She went back into the kitchen stuffed the will into the fire and watched it burn. She stepped back out into the sunlight. "I don't know why you're all just standing there. You will have a bride and groom to welcome into the house soon. That normally involves a party of some sort."

Her words seemed to prod people back to life. Slowly people started to turn, to look at each other, some even started to speak, but then lapsed into silence. Maljie beckoned to me to follow her, and she walked solemnly through the assembled group and out onto the road. There we continued in the direction we had been travelling in. After a while I asked her, "How much of that was Grandmother and how much was you?"

"She told me what had happened and asked me how we could fix it. I promised her we would fix it. It broke the old lady's heart to see those two young people kept apart because the generation above wasn't willing to own its own mistakes."

"Well hopefully you've fixed it."

"The will is fair. Everybody is provided for. Nobody should have reason to complain."

We walked along for a little while, then I said, "Telbat Spurt was right, you'd make an excellent Patriarch." And then I skipped to one side to avoid the fist swinging for my head.

Chapter 14

Blackthorn Tower was one of the less prepossessing keeps that I've seen in my time. It was really a four storey house, the first three stories stone-built, the windows mere arrow slits. The top storey was a more conventional dwelling with quite large bow windows. It had a flat roof and the top of the tower had a parapet and two men with crossbows watched us incuriously as we walked along the road towards them.

The tower itself was surrounded by a wall. This was little more than eight feet tall and seemed to be designed to stop livestock straying. Outside the wall was a small village. The houses were single storey cottages, stone built and whitewashed. Each had a fenced vegetable patch, and to the south of us stretched fields of grain. There was one gateway into the tower courtyard and the gate was ajar. A guard leaning against it provided security. Once through the gate you were in a courtyard. The perimeter wall was lined with low buildings. There was no real wall walk, you'd have to stand on a building roof. The tower was at the far side of the courtyard. Barnyard fowl fussed and gleaned their way around, one man was holding a horse whilst another was working on a shoe.

The guard at the gate asked our business and we explained we wished to see Fargwurt, Lord Blackthorn. The guard gestured towards to tower. "Go in, he'll decide whether he wants to see you or not."

The tower door was at first floor level, reached by a set of stone steps. It's a traditional enough design, it means that the attackers cannot use a battering ram to break down the door and must proceed in single file to get to the door. Above the steps is a larger than normal arrow slit, just the right size for pouring a bucket of boiling water or hot sand.

This means the ground floor has to be reached from

within the tower and is used mainly for storage. Whether of agricultural surplus or prisoners depends entirely on the nature of the business conducted by the lord of the tower.

It is a system with obvious martial advantages and equally obvious domestic disadvantages. Everything has to be carried up one narrow set of stairs, through a narrow door, and down another set of stairs into the ground floor store. In this case, the owner of the tower had succumbed to the realities of the situation. There was a large door set into tower at ground level. It was made of heavy timbers and had a large lock. It was wide enough to back a cart through.

We walked up the steps. Once inside we were directed to a waiting room next to the door. This was a cubby hole with no chairs. It did have an arrow slit and I suspect it was a guard point. Eventually we were summoned to the third floor. There, in a hall which took up perhaps most of the floor area of the tower, sat Fargwurt, Lord of Blackthorn Tower.

Frankly I was not impressed. I've seen Port Naain usurers or actuaries who would cut a better figure as a Partannese lordling. Fargwurt was fat, grubby and was wearing mis-matched bits salvaged from several expensive suits of armour. None of them were really in his size. Perhaps because people of his size rarely wear armour.

His lieutenants were more impressive, but there again, I suspect at this point, Maljie in her robes as a maiden penitent looked more warlike than Fargwurt. Sitting around the room on wooden benches were another dozen men. I guessed they were Fargwurt's minions. After all I could imagine no other reason for allowing them to come armed into his presence. Most of them would be banished from the ranks of any but the most disreputable Port Naain crime syndicate for offensive slovenliness. A collection of dunnykin divers, armed with weaponry and armour they had discovered during their labours, would have the self-respect to attempt to look better than this rabble did.

Maljie marched into the middle of the room and looked round. Then she glanced at a piece of paper in her hand.

"So you are Fargwurt. That means you," here she turned to the taller lieutenant, "must be Rattledrain, and you," here she turned to the second lieutenant, "must be Gorangle."

Everybody was somewhat put out by this. Even some of the minions ceased masticating or hunting for fleas and stared at Maljie.

Rattledrain cracked first. "Yes, I am Rattledrain." Maljie once more checked her piece of paper. "Ah yes, wanted in Port Naain for champerty, reckless endangerment, barratry, and obscene libel. Total assets in deposit box, one hundred and forty-seven alars, a bag of sixty-three vintenars, a matching pair of gold candlesticks, gem encrusted; and a pottery jar full of rings and miscellaneous costume jewellery of limited value."

She turned to the other lieutenant. "And you, Gorangle, are wanted in Port Naain for effecting a public mischief and fraudulent conversion. Also wanted in Prae Ducis for Seditious libel, and in Avitas for embracery and petty treason. Total assets in deposit box, two hundred and twelve alars, twelve vintenars and a clay pot full of low denomination brass dregs of miscellaneous minting. There is also a nice seventy piece silver Cutlery Set, three large silver tureens and two silver condiment sets, (described here as erotic masterpieces)."

She then turned finally to Fargwurt. "And you are wanted in Port Naain for cheating, forgery, misprision of felony; in Avitas for embracery and being a common scold. Also you are wanted in Prae Ducis for forcible detainer, conspiracy to corrupt the public morals, lèse-majesté..." Maljie stopped, "How do you commit lèse-majesté in a republic?" She sounded genuinely perplexed. "Never mind, I'm not sure I want to know. Also you have two safe deposit boxes, one contains a small bag of hack-silver, valued at four alars. The other is empty."

Fargwurt almost exploded, "It's not empty, it's got a lot of money in it."

"Had. You sent your mistress to withdraw money to hire fighters for some scheme or the other. She withdrew the money and instead purchased a pleasant enough house and a baker's shop just off Ropewalk."

She looked round. The minions were without exception staring at her in almost open-mouthed stupefaction. "I don't think much of your hospitality here. Gorangle, isn't there a chair for a lady?"

Gorangle moved uncertainly from one foot to another. "Courtesy would indicate that the lady did at least vouchsafe us a name."

"Sorry, I am Maljie."

One of the minions, unprompted, brought a chair and rubbed the seat with his grubby sleeve as he carried it across. Maljie bestowed upon him a charming smile and sat down.

"So Fargwurt. You're in deep trouble, barely have the money to pay your men and once word gets out, the vultures will start to circle. If I were you, I'd hand over Brother Tanai, we'll be on our way and if you're quick about it, we might even be able to put in a good word for you."

I had been watching Fargwurt carefully. He obviously hadn't know about his mistress making off with his money. To be fair it was news to me as well, but having never knowingly met his mistress I felt I could be excused the oversight. But rather than becoming despondent he was growing more and more angry. Given that he was ostentatiously corpulent and unfit I did wonder whether he would have some sort of seizure. Instead he exploded verbally.

"Guards, dump them in the dungeon with that blasted monk. I'll get my money back by selling the three of them to their friends in Port Naain."

Somewhat hesitantly, Rattledrain said, "Is that entirely wise, Fargwurt. It is Maljie you're talking about."

Gorangle added, "She knows too much."

Fargwurt was standing up now, he was almost dancing with frustration. "Look, don't try thinking, you're not cut out for it. Look where it's got you so far." He turned and pointed to two of the most gormless looking minions. "You two, grab these and dump them in the dungeon."

As they shambled across and grabbed us, Fargwurt added, "I have no doubt that Rattledrain will be so kind as to unlock the door for you so you can thrust them in. Won't you Rattledrain." There was a great deal of emphasis on the last sentence.

Rattledrain led us from the hall and down the stairs. He took us outside, down the narrow steps and round to the large door on the ground floor. This he unlocked. "We pass food down through the trapdoor, but frankly it's a lot less fuss letting people in and out this way."

The two minions thrust us through the open door. As I was going through the door Rattledrain shouted, "Stop." He reached out. "What are you hiding in your cowl?"

I was surprised by this. "Nothing."

He put his hand in to check and then said, "Push them through and shut the door."

📖📖📖

The inside of the 'dungeon' wasn't as dark as I expected. A monk, who I assumed to be Brother Tanai, was sitting on some sacks of grain watching us. In case there might be room for doubt, he introduced himself. "Good afternoon, I am Tanai. It appears that fat-gut Fargwurt has taken to collecting members of religious orders."

"I am Maljie and this is Tallis. The Patriarch was worried about you and sent us to find you and to take you to Port Naain."

Dryly, Tanai commented, "Well you've certainly found me."

I had noticed an unexpected weight in my cowl. As Maljie and Tanai talked, I tried to explore the depths of the cowl, without just raising it. The last thing I wanted was to precipitate whatever some joker had put there down the back of my neck.

Eventually I realised that both Maljie and Tanai were watching me with puzzled expressions. Finally I managed to extract from my cowl a heavy metal key. "I think Rattledrain put it in."

Maljie nodded. "Good, it will make things easier."

"Why, what happens next?"

"Our friends arrive, explain how it's all an unfortunate mistake, and we leave."

Tanai asked, "And when do your friends arrive?"

"It'll be early morning, before dawn. So now Tallis can let them in. Try the key, it'll probably be to the outside door."

I tried it and it was, I relocked the door. Maljie pointed up the set of steps that led to the trapdoor. "Now we need that open."

She climbed the stairs and hammered on the trap. It opened and a particularly gormless face looked down at her. "Yeah?"

"Let me past please, I have to go to the privy."

"What?"

"Well you cannot expect a lady to do it down there surrounded by men?"

It was obvious that the guard had never encountered this situation before. "Well yer best foller me."

Maljie disappeared through the trap door. Perhaps half an hour later she reappeared.

"Gentlemen, I've told this gentleman that if he leaves the trap unlocked, neither of you two will take advantage of the situation."

Tanai and I looked at each other, somewhat bemused by the turn of events.

I said, "Certainly not."

"I too promise not to go up the stairs."

"Thank you gentlemen, I was sure I could rely upon you."

The guard looked relieved. "Yeah, that's good. What wi us not having a key for the trap no more. I has to put my chair on it an' sit on it to hold it down. Gives mi the willies sitting over an 'ole."

Maljie smiled benignly at him. "Oh how terrible for you."

"Yeah an' they meks a big fuss about it an' all. So I tell't them, sod you lot, I said, I'm not shifting this bluidy chair all't time. Yer can tek yer bluidy prisoners in through't t'other door."

Maljie once more smiled at him and then majestically descended the stairs. It has to be admitted that the robes of a maiden penitent seemed to have been designed to allow the wearer to descend stairs with sweeping dignity. "Then I suggest we three get some sleep."

📖📖📖

It was dark when Maljie prodded me. "Wake up, it's time for you to go and let our friends in."

I got to my feet and felt for the key. The door unlocked easily enough and I opened it a little and looked around. The courtyard was in darkness and was totally silent. I made my way towards the gate. In these circumstances it is as well to act as if you have no doubts as to whether you're doing the right thing. At the gate itself I could see it was held closed by three large wooden bars which dropped into metal supports. They weren't too heavy and I lifted them out of the supports and put them down on the ground out of the way. I carefully tugged the gate and it slowly came open.

Almost immediately the face of Orwan Bullip appeared. I'd known him since I was a child. I stepped back and Orwan, in half armour and with his sword drawn, stepped through the gate. He was followed by Little Toddy, Dillup, Mad Dog, and Niblo.

They were in his 'gang' when they were boys and they'd stuck together over the years. Orwan shook my hand, "Good to meet you again, Tallis my lad. Apparently you're to get us into the tower."

"Yes, follow me."

I led them across the courtyard to the open door. When I glanced back, I could see that Orwan had gathered together a fair band, there must have been a score of men following him. Once in the tower I could see the trap door was open, Maljie stood on the top and beckoned Orwan and his men upwards. Silently like so many hunting feroce, they moved like shadows up the stairs and disappeared into the tower.

Maljie said, "Right, we make our way back to Chatterfield, the Elusive should be loaded by now and the captain promised he'd wait until this evening's tide."

I asked, "But Orwan?"

"He and his friends are getting a bit old for mercenary service, so were looking to retire. Blackthorn Tower has quite a lot of good arable land attached to it. I'll not say he'll become a gentleman farmer, but I'll square things with the Municipality of Chatterfield. They'll be happy to recognise his claim, he'll be a damned sight better neighbour than Fargwurt."

As we walked towards Chatterfield, Tanai spoke. He had been thinking. "So what actually is going on? Have I been rescued as part of some shoddy Port Naain usurer extortion scheme?"

"How do you mean?"

"You'll have seen it as often as I have, Maljie. A usurer puts up some cash, their thug hires other thugs, takes over an existing operation and the usurer skims off a nice profit."

I felt I had to chip in. "Orwan isn't that sort of thug. I've known him pretty much all my life. He grew up with the others on the streets of Port Naain, and rather than drift into organised crime, he led his band south as baggage guards for one of the short lived

infantry companies that go down into Partann.
Anyway they survived and kept surviving. I followed
his career if only because they'd send packets of
letters back to assorted mothers and I would be the
one summoned to read the letters. They're hard lads,
but they're decent enough hard lads."

Tanai said, "Well anybody in that trade who
remembers to send letters back to their mother..."

"Along with the occasional cash and trinkets which
brightened a sister's trousseau or paid for an old
lady's visit to the doctor."

"So what is behind this? I can see it being a useful
retirement scheme for an aging mercenary with a
heart of gold, but why were you trying to rescue me
in the first place?"

Maljie spoke for the first time in this conversation.
"Simple, the Patriarch wanted you in Port Naain."

"Why?"

"Because you are to be the next patriarch."

"You are, of course, joking."

Maljie passed him a letter, which Tanai read aloud.
"'To our beloved companion in the service of Aea, we
wish you to return to Port Naain and succeed us as
patriarch'......" He looked up. "It then goes on to heap
nebulous and unspecified praise on the recipient of
the letter." He paused again. "To our beloved
companion? That's as near as you can get to saying,
'To whomsoever it may concern' without in fact using
the words."

Tanai stopped in the road, "Basically you have been
sent to get another Patriarch and they're not sure
who is going to be fool enough to take the job, so
they gave you a suitably bland letter you could give
to anybody."

Personally I was with Tanai in this. The letter did
seem to show a lack of faith in our abilities to
persuade him.

Maljie said, "So you don't want to take on the role?"
She managed to sound shocked. Given that she was
still the first choice of both Patriarchs, I could imagine

her being somewhat put out by it all.

"I have no intention of taking on the role, I have too much work to do here."

Maljie asked, "What do you mean, work to do here?"

"Assuming you are right about Orwan Bullip, then there is much to do. Firstly if I talk to him and agree with your assessment, I can introduce him to the Municipality, and without boasting, my opinion will carry more weight with them than that of somebody just down from Port Naain. Secondly he'll need somebody to guide him through the various political undercurrents in the area. Then with a civilised Lord in place, I can start doing my job properly."

Maljie looked at him, I wondered if she was assessing whether together we could overpower him and carry him back to Port Naain. "You're sure about this, think of the good you could do as Patriarch"

"In twenty or thirty years, who knows, but now I have work to do." He bowed to Maljie and then to me. "So thank you for your intervention in the situation. I promise to be grateful once I've got order restored." With that he turned and walked back towards Blackthorn Tower.

Maljie watched him go. "Bugger."

Chapter 15

Our trip back was uneventful. I was put ashore at Candleman's Cove along with a large consignment of contraband that would then travel to Port Naain via somewhat more devious routes. I chose Candleman's Cove because a number of my clients would be spending at least part of the summer there. This meant I could catch up with them and their various trials and tribulations.

But it also gave me the chance of catching up with

Port Naain gossip, admittedly at one remove; and of course it meant I wasn't present at the shrine when Maljie had to report that our mission had failed. Obviously being the one who wasn't there, I was the obvious recipient for the blame, but I'd probably be blamed anyway and at least this way I was being blamed in my absence. To be fair, looking at the various alternatives, if I am to be blamed, I prefer not to be there. People always claim that it's unfair to be tried in one's absence, but at least if you don't like the verdict you need never go back.

At Candleman's Cove I made my way to the Assembly Rooms and entered the Grand Rout by the simple expedient of gesturing vaguely behind me to a group who were following. I had left my mendicant's robes with Maljie in the Elusive and was thus my elegant self. Admittedly I might have been a little soiled due to arriving in an open boat and having to help unload barrels of whelks onto the beach but still, such things are expected of a gentleman along this coast and nobody would think the worse of me because of it. Almost immediately I started to meet people I knew. Some of them knew I was supposed to be in Partann. Indeed Madam Dorca had apparently been quite concerned. She beckoned me across.

"Tallis, if I'd known your time in Partann was to be spent in the north I would have worried less."

I bowed. "I have been a little further south, but hurried north when I realised I had a chance to meet up with so many friends here."

"Apparently there have been terrible deeds done. Do you remember Orwan Bullip?"

"Yes, I've known him on and off for a long time."

"His mother used to clean for my mother and I've always had a soft spot for him, but still. Apparently he's led an army of desperados into Uttermost Partann, and they've stormed and sacked a great keep down there. There are rumours of hundreds dead and Orwan is now a great lord among the Partannese."

"I cannot have been in the same area, Madam Dorca. Even a poet would have noticed something like that." But there was other news worth keeping an ear open for as well. It was Madam Halwhistle and her circle who mentioned that the Grand Slide would be opened.

For those who don't know Port Naain, the Grand Slide is 'an occasion' and frankly, great fun. When there is enough snow, (which doesn't happen every year) the Sinecurists will announce that a slide will be held. Then all those wishing to take part will assemble on Sinecurists Walk. They run down the Walk, pushing their sledge before them, and turn into New Gallows Prospect. Whereas the Walk is level, the Prospect starts a slow descent. But then you turn off into Lame Pauper's Ginnel. This narrow street descends rapidly, and towards the bottom, cuts across a couple of other, lesser known lanes; changing its own name as it does so. Finally it debouches onto Ropewalk. The Sinecurists have sturdy men with staffs close off those streets which cross the track of the Grand Slide which can then proceed at a breakneck pace whilst limiting the chance of wreaking havoc amongst innocent bystanders.

As I listened to the discussion it suddenly struck me that people were talking as if the Grand Slide was going to happen within the next month. To be frank I wasn't sanguine about the chances of us getting snow during the summer. I listened more closely and even asked gently leading questions. Finally it was Calina Salin who explained things to me.

"It's simple, Tallis. The Patriarchs suggested it."

"Why, are they going to make it snow in summer?"

I was graced with the look sisters and daughters reserve for the males of their family who are undoubtedly incapable of rational thought."

"No, they suggested that the surface of Lame Pauper's Ginnel be covered with something slippery."

Another thing occurred to me, "Why are the Patriarchs suddenly getting involved in this sort of thing?"

At this point Calina moved closer to me and spoke more softly. "Well because there are two of them, they get through the jobs that must be done in half the time. Then they put off the jobs that will wait, 'until we have a patriarch.' Finally from what I was told, they were driving your incumbent mad, getting under her feet, asking questions about everything. So she asked Laxey to get them out of the shrine. So he's had them visiting those houses where ladies have 'open house' for good causes in the afternoon. This led to them getting invitations to attend evening events and apparently they're now quite the toast of society. Apparently late one evening somebody commented that we haven't had a Grand Slide for years. Then because both Patriarchs appear to be considering moving away from Port Naain once their successor is appointed, it was felt a pity that they missed seeing one. So it was decided by somebody that we'd have one."

I felt rising panic. "So this is one of those things that seems like an excellent idea at one o-clock in the morning when everybody has finished with wine and has moved on to spirits!"

"Something like that." Calina admitted.

"I'm not sure whether to steal a horse and ride to Port Naain now to try and salvage something, or steal a horse, abandon you all to your just desserts, and ride south to see if Orwan Bullip needs a court poet."

"I'm not sure why you're so worried about it, Tallis. It's not as if you were there."

"Calina, I will walk into the shrine and one or more Patriarchs will casually say, "Oh, Tallis is here. He's the perfect person to organise it.""

"In which case, I'd steal the horse and ride north and do it now. Orwan Bullip is a chap I have a lot of time for, but I suspect he's happier with fart jokes and comic songs than romantic poetry."

📖📖📖

As it was I didn't have to steal a horse. I managed to get a seat on a cart that had brought a load of Partannese whelks from Port Naain. Obviously Partannese whelks are far more toothsome than the whelks one harvests from the seas off Port Naain. But to protect Port Naain interests there is considerable duty to pay on Partannese whelks. Thus they are smuggled.

So when the management of the Assembly Rooms in Candleman's Cove wish to purchase whelks to put on the menu, they will contact their favoured dealer of illicit whelks in Port Naain and the dealer will send them a cart load of whelks. The carter delivering the whelks from Port Naain then collected the whelks I had helped unload onto the beach, and I rode with him back to Port Naain where we unloaded his cart at the back of a nondescript house, two streets behind Ropewalk. Next day, if the Assembly Rooms has a demand for more whelks then the barrels will be loaded back onto the cart and will travel once more to Candleman's Cove. I too struggle to understand the system, but then I am a poet and thus is expected to have only limited comprehension of these deep financial matters.

Still whatever the ins and outs of the system, it got me home to Port Naain. I made my way to the barge and as Shena was still out I sent her a message by a convenient street child that I was home, and prepared our evening repast, whelks cooked gently in a white wine sauce poured over a loaf of today's bread I had managed to purchase from a bakery despairing of disposing of all its stock so late in the day.

As we ate and brought each other up-to-date with our various activities there was a knock on the door. I opened the door with the casual confidence of a man who has been out of town and therefore cannot be guilty of anything. Standing there was my cousin Thela, the temple dancer.

I stepped back to welcome her in and started to prepare coffee for the three of us. Thela was not disposed to casual small talk but instead came straight to the point.

"Tallis, why is Maljie cultivating Sister Alanette?"

"Is she? I've just got back to Port Naain."

"Well Maljie got home the day before you and can have been barely off the boat before descended on the shrine and sought out the Sister."

I was in something of a predicament. My cousin Thela is my nearest family. Indeed she's probably the only family I have who deigns to notice me, and I am immensely fond of her. "Thela, I can tell you but you must keep it a secret."

"You know me, Tallis, I don't gossip."

"It's simple. The Patriarchs want Sister Alanette to be the next Patriarch."

Thela looked at me thoughtfully for a moment and then said with absolute certainty. "She won't take the position."

"That's Maljie's problem not mine."

"Maljie would make an excellent Patriarch, why doesn't she do it."

"Because she doesn't want the job either, Thela." There was silence as I passed around mugs of coffee, then Thela said, "You'd make a good Patriarch."

"Me?"

"Yes, you could read the various lessons of the day perfectly, you're the ideal person for stage-managing the great formal occasions and you could deliver your sermons in verse, which would allow you to sidestep all the great theological controversies."

"Well I don't want the job. But more importantly why doesn't Sister Alanette want it?"

"She's far too busy. She's trying to raise the money to build an extension so we can house more orphans."

"I thought you already took orphans."

"Girls only. And we have to make the pretence that they're in training as temple dancers."

For a brief moment the artist in my beloved cousin surfaced, "Tallis, if you knew the amount of time I waste teaching leaden footed, tone deaf children with no grasp of time or rhythm..."

She pulled herself together. "Sister Alanette has a plan. She wants to acquire or build half a dozen cottages. There you'd have couples bring up the children as their own. We could take boys and girls and they'd get a more appropriate education."

Shena commented, "It sounds a good idea."

I was silent, an idea had occurred to me. "If we could raise this money, get the project underway, then there might be a chance Sister Alanette would consider being Patriarch?"

Thela sounded doubtful. "Well there's a chance. I'll not say it was a good one."

"With Maljie and two Patriarchs working on her, it might be the best chance we've got, and at the very least we'll raise the money she needs."

📖📖📖

The following morning I made my way to the Shrine of Aea in her Aspect as the Personification of Tempered Enthusiasm. I was in good time for what was grandly called, 'The Daily Chapter Meeting.' This has been characterised as 'the drink coffee and bewail our fate session.' In this case the company was more exalted than usual. Both Patriarchs were present, having nothing to do and plenty of time to do it in.

I had been giving a lot of thought to how to raise money. I have no doubt that Maljie could get some through her contacts, but I suspected we might need more.

As I sat down and reached for the mug of coffee Laxey pushed in my direction, I said, "I see our two Patriarchs have decided to have a Grand Slide this summer."

Patriarch Sydna looked at Patriarch Telbat. "Well neither of us have seen it for years and it's unlikely we'll ever see it again, so it seemed a good idea at the time."

"It's just that if we want Sister Alanette to be the next Patriarch, the easy way is probably to raise the money so she can set up her scheme for looking after orphans. If, whilst working with her in this, you cannot convince her to take the job, then neither of you is the man I take you for."

Maljie immediately spotted the opportunity. "So how much money does she need to raise?"

I shrugged. "You'll have to ask her, but I suspect it'll take you speaking sweetly to usurers and others of the criminal classes, at the same time we'll work out how to make money on the Grand Slide."

Laxey asked, "But who is organising the Grand Slide."

"Annually somebody purchases the Sinecure, 'Master of the Snows.' Given we rarely have snow in the first half of winter and the Sinecurists take up their posts at the Winter Solstice, the Master or Mistress of the Snows will be pretty sure by now that the money they paid will just go into the common pot and they'll get no kudos for their pains. So I can see them being happy enough to support this Grand Slide. Indeed if our Patriarchs offer to help run it, I cannot see them objecting."

"But how much money can we raise on children just sliding down hill?"

I was beginning to sense the potential grandeur of our project. "I think we have to extend things. Because there is no snow people were talking about pouring lard down Lame Pauper's Ginnel. But the damned stuff would be there for months and it would make it a death trap. What if, instead of a sledge, people had a small cart on four wheels they steered? Also what if we extended the course, so that you had somebody who pulled the cart, as well as the person driving it. So you'd start at the Chamber of the Council of Sinecurists. Then at Lame Pauper's Ginnel, the person pulling would have to leap aboard, then at the bottom they'd pull the cart back up a chosen route to the Council Building again?"

The ideas came thick and fast.

"Would you have entry fees?"

"And we could take a cut from the bookies by allowing them to set their stalls up."

The Deacon had been quiet, sketching on a piece of scrap paper. "I think I've got a plan for your cart. Low slung, with four small wheels, the front two steering. The body will have to be long enough for two people to sit on."

"Not too low slung, we'll have ladies riding these in the height of fashion who want to look their best."

"We will?" The Deacon looked somewhat surprised.

"Well you always do, almost whatever you organise." Maljie broke into our deliberations. "These are details, we have to get the appropriate Sinecurist to support us first. Does anybody know who it is?"

Given that the meeting was being held in the elegantly refurbished library, I reached for the shrine's copy of Lantram's 'The Sinecurists of Naain'. I confess that each year I attempt to acquire a copy for my own use and each year I add in scores of separate pages of scribbled notes. These detail who is feuding with whom, which lady is currently friends with which lady, where people stand on the great issues of the day, and who is having an affair with whom. Also useful is information such as who is rumoured to be facing financial difficulties, or alternatively has come into money. All the information a jobbing poet really needs.

I flicked through to the appropriate page, "Maintainer of the lesser drains; Malversation, prevention of; Mascarons, maintaining the quality of; here we are, Master of the Snows. Maljie, you're in luck, this year it is Thespan Slackwater."

"Is he the father of Almas Slackwater?" Maljie was already looking more positive.

"He is indeed. Hopefully I shall see Almas at the Silverthwaite 'At Home' I'm helping organise this evening.

I've heard rumours that she intends to gate-crash the event. If I do get to see her, I have no doubt Thespan will be contracting you tomorrow to see about the details of organising the event."

I confess here that I hadn't been entirely honest with Maljie. I hadn't heard rumours that Almas intended to gate-crash the Silverthwaite 'At Home.' I had in reality pleaded with her to do it.

This requires further elucidation. Madam Silverthwaite is a nice lady. Her husband is a pleasant enough fellow who is happy to let her entertain as she will. Her circle of acquaintance is composed largely of similar ladies. All with children who have left home, all with husbands who are safely ensconced in the middle reaches of their professions with worthy but rather dull interests. None of these ladies is going to be found surrounded by admirers drinking cheap sparkling wine from her shoes. None is going to dance naked as she bursts out of a giant cake. But if I mention to them a young woman I know who is struggling with a child who has difficulties, then action will be taken. They do not merely give money (because in all candour they don't have a lot of it) but instead one of them will turn up and help. Madam Silverthwaite herself looks after one small boy, five mornings a week. She sits with him, and after many struggles and setbacks has taught him to read. Now she shares with him a world of fantasy and delight. Together they read fifty-dreg tales of improbable adventures in Partann and even more distant places. They read them companionably, taking turns, a chapter each.

Now you might ask why Madam Silverthwaite needs me to organise her various events. In all honesty, she doesn't, but I am hired in the hope I will bring to the event a touch of reckless abandon, of exoticism, almost of surprise and danger. Obviously this is never stated as such, but we both know it. Thus invitations to an evening with Madam Silverthwaite are keenly awaited by the ladies in her circle and I would suffer much rather than let those ladies down.

Hence I had asked Almas Slackwater to gate-crash the event. Almas is charming, pretty, at least a generation younger than the guests, and has been described in my presence as maenadic. I would prefer 'winsome' but would go so far as to admit 'frenetic.' She also wishes to be a performance poet. Hence I sent a note begging her to gate-crash. I hadn't the faintest idea how she would do it but I could trust her to do it in a manner that would provide Madam Silverthwaite and her friends the sort of evening they would delight in.

Chapter 16

I arrived early to be greeted by Madam Silverthwaite and we ran once more through the arrangements. I had arranged for her cook to spend an afternoon with Margarita, Maljie's younger sister. She makes an excellent lemon drizzle cake, and now Madam Silverthwaite's cook had learned the secrets sitting at her feet. (Or perhaps more correctly, peering at her mixing bowl) But of such little things are social triumphs made.

The other guests arrived, people chatted over glasses of infusion, and the lemon drizzle cake was much admired. Cook, Aea love her, was so pleased to be summoned to the parlour to be widely commended, that she set aside a goodly chunk for Shena and I to share. Then, when I was about to introduce the more formal part of the programme (a short recitation and I knew one or two of the ladies would be happy to sing a song or two) the maid appeared.

"Madam, there's a blind soothsaying woman at the door as wants to speak to you."

I admired the maid. She managed to give the impression that such persons were regular visitors, whilst giving absolutely no hint as to whether she believed in the authenticity of the soothsayers' visions.

Madam managed not to glance at me, and said, "Well bring her in please."

The maid returned with a thin, stooped woman, long hair hanging down, almost obscuring her face. A lot of her face was obscured by the bandage she wore over her eyes.

Madam Silverthwaite asked, "I confess you have the advantage of me. I am Madam Silverthwaite. Who are you?"

"Bursiss, seventh daughter of Nissa, seventh daughter of Ma. I was told to come here in a vision. The spirits led me through the streets to your door.

Why?
Aea knows, but tends not to lightly divulge
Reasons
No wanton to casually promulge
Her thoughts.
Let me meet the company in solitary state
Then
Privily I can peer through the account books of fate
I crave
That my whims you kindly indulge

Madam Silverthwaite whispered to me, "A blind soothsayer, how romantic. Only a maiden on a white palfrey led by a dwarf could cap this."

I leaned forward and whispered back. "I could create a booth for her with a clothes horse and some old blankets."

"Do it please."

Ten minutes later the soothsayer was sitting in her booth. I'd set the clothes horse up in the little parlour. Draping two blankets over it produced a tent of sorts and I'd put in two chairs with a small table between them. On the table was a candle, for the visitor. Obviously a blind soothsayer didn't need it. Over the next hour or so Madam's guests would drift quietly into the booth, would introduce themselves and the soothsayer would hold their hands for a few moments and then pronounce a short but cryptic verse concerning their future. The lady would frantically write down these words of wisdom (I ended up leaving my indelible pencil and some torn up envelopes for those who hadn't got a notebook in their handbag) so they had something to ponder later. I only remember one verse,

> I see, without seeing
> Beauty hidden but shining still,
> Glowing like hidden fire
> A spirit that only love can distil.

Now the lady who was given that was admittedly a little plain. But still, she was never less than delightful company. I believe her confidence was greatly boosted by the verse. Indeed her husband mentioned in passing a week or two later that to his delight she was carrying herself like the lady he knew she was, rather than as the lady she saw in the mirror. Eventually the guests had all meet the soothsayer and I too slipped in.

"Good evening, Almas."

"Was my disguise so easy to see through, Tallis?"

"If you use it again, give more thought to your hair. I know few blind seers but their hair is either tightly bound or cut short. Careless abandon takes far too much arranging."

She smiled wryly. "How did it go?"

"Well everybody seems to have enjoyed the evening. That is always a good start."

"Did Madam mention I called to see her?"

This surprised me. "No, she said nothing."

"Well I felt to do the job properly I needed to know who was coming, so we went through the guest list and discussed them, and I would do the verse for each."

"Wise." I produced a piece of paper from my pocket. "And now I have another project. We're thinking of doing the Grand Slide, this month. As your father is Master of the Snows he really ought to get involved, if only as the figurehead. Anyway I produced a few notes for you, as I ought to get back to the guests." Almas moved her bandage slightly and looked at the notes in candle light. "This sounds as if it could be immense fun. I shall have words with my father when I get home."

"I hoped you would."

📖📖📖

Obviously all the planning involved endless tedious meetings, all sorts of worthy people had to be brought into the process. Not for anything they offered, but so their egos could be lovingly polished and Maljie could then ask them for money for Sister Alanette and her charitable work. Sister Alanette also had to be ensnared within the spreading tentacles of the organisation. But that sort of organising I could leave to Maljie. To me fell a far more difficult task. There are people whose support was needed not because they would become generous benefactors, but because their support would ensure our event was considered fashionable. Thus society would throw itself behind us. Now whilst some of these individuals get on well enough, some do not. I hold up the examples of Mesdames Halgan and Malwin. If they smiled upon us and mentioned us in glowing terms to their respective circles of friends and acquaintances, we could expect to prosper with their support. On the other hand, for them to frown upon our efforts was not even to be contemplated.

Both were leading lights in the Port Naain Society of Anonymous Lady Philanthropists. Both could be relied upon to be polite to each other, indeed at events where they turned up they would act as if the other was a bosom friend.

Yet Madam Halgan described Madam Malwin to me with the words, "A more deeply devious woman never drew breath, nobody trusts her." On the other hand Madam Malwin pointed out Madam Halgan to me and said, "Never trust her, nobody else does. A more sly and devious woman never lived."

The problem with having them both in a meeting was not that they would fight, but that they would so neutralise each other as to mean that we got nothing from either of them. Yet we had to invite both. To invite only one would put us firmly on one side of this conflict. This would give us all of the disadvantages and none of the advantages of their participation.

The way to deal with this matter was to ensure than only one of them came to a meeting. So when we had the date arranged I had to go round my circle of most trusted patrons, pleading with them to invite one or the other of the two ladies to be the guest of honour, giving a little talk about some charitable cause she was interested in.

Now this seems simple enough, but it all got terribly complicated. For example, the Widow Handwill promised she would invite Madam Halgan to talk to a select group of friends about some of the causes the Port Naain Society of Anonymous Lady Philanthropists supports. Unfortunately Madam Mudfold had released a new range of dresses for the autumn and the Widow had half promised Madam Mudfold that she could bring some of her dresses and exhibit those on the chosen evening. So I then had to visit Madan Mudfold and put my problem to her. Instead of an evening with the Widow Handwill, I promised her that Suzaine Gicken would take things in hand for her. Suzaine is the granddaughter of a sadly deceased patron of mine, the late, great, Mistress Hanchkillian. Now Suzaine didn't have the Hanchkillian money behind her, although I suspect her grandmother would not have forgotten her. But she had eventually married Silac Gicken who ran Gickens' Printers. Suzaine produced a monthly periodical which looked at fashion and society. Bitter experience had taught her that whilst gossip and tittle-tattle could earn you remarkable amounts of money from sales, it was easier for everybody to play it safe and just give people elegant clothing.

Still, I made my way to the print shop. There I found Suzaine and Silac setting up the type for a collection of essays from Tilia Veel. She is perhaps the best of the younger generation of essayists (faint praise, so perhaps I should say that nobody of her generation writes prose like she does) and she was present to oversee the setting of the type. This she was doing by playing with Suzaine and Silac's twin daughters and their puppy.

I explained my predicament, Suzaine promised to help and gave me a note to deliver to Madam Mudfold, asking when it would be convenient for Suzaine to send an artist to sketch some of the dresses. But of course Tilia Veel couldn't help overhearing and I was left feeling that I will feature, in a small way, in one of her essays in the future. I did my best to ensure she would remember me warmly by enquiring about when her essays were to be published and asked Silac for details so that I could share them with my patrons.

Ensuring one lady missed one meeting took me the best part of a day and left me exhausted. Rather than return to the shrine to report on my success, instead I went to the Misanthropes, where I collapsed in an arm chair with a large glass of white wine. At least there nobody was going to say, brightly, 'Well seeing as how you're doing nothing Tallis, could you just…..'

📖📖📖

I must have drifted off to sleep because I opened my eyes to see a damned big dog staring at me. Now it's not that dogs are banned from the Misanthropes. Indeed most are better behaved than the usual clientele which is largely poets on this floor and usurers' clerks downstairs.

But most poets don't own a dog.

Given that most of us can barely afford to feed ourselves, a dog is a step too far. Also if a poet does have a dog, cutting remarks are often made along the lines that the dog is obviously the sensible, thinking member of the partnership. Most poets feel that it is unfair to subject a dog to this sort of pressure.

I recognised the dog as 'Spot'. Tiffy's escort. I glanced round and Tiffy was indeed sitting in the next chair, browsing a copy of the Port Naain Intelligencer that was at least a week old. She saw me stir.

"I've been looking for you, Tallis. Shena said that you'd be here. Apparently because of the tide, she'll be working and you are expected to fend for yourself this evening."

Thinking about it, Shena and I had agreed on this first thing that morning. I'd totally forgotten.

Tiffy continued. "Anyway Shena said that I could take you to dine at the Great Gusto."

This was a positive development. I enjoy the Great Gusto but I can never afford to eat there. Then Tiffy added, "I've been talking to your cousin..."

Here she was obviously trying to remember a name, because she then said, "Thela".

I relaxed again, I have a number of cousins but Thela I could trust to accentuate the positive.

"But we can discuss her comments over a meal."

It was as we left that we had problems. Trane Forsgill appeared at the top of the stairs and immediately started to introduce himself to Tiffy. Trane calls himself a poet, but there again if he could play the guitar he would call himself a troubadour and if he could find a lady willing to support him financially he would become a gigolo. The problem is that once he'd halted us, a number of others joined us. Their presence irritated Trane Forsgill, but it irritated Tiffy and me more and Spot was getting distinctly annoyed.

I looked round, I had to do something. I suspect that Tiffy and Spot would be regarded as my guests (even though anybody can walk in off the street) and I would be held responsible if Spot ate anybody on the premises. I noted a bucket of paint and a long handled brush. One of the staff was painting the landing ceiling and was rearranging the sheets he'd put down to protect the carpet.

I said, "Trane, be a good fellow and move along, I have to escort this lady to a meeting."

"Steelyard, run along and pander to the whims of a rich widow or something."

It was probably at this point that my original idea of a measured response, pleading lack of time, the need to get everybody out of the way before Spot lost his temper, and similar sensible measures was abandoned. I may indeed have over-reacted. But still, Trane had barely finished speaking before I caught him full in the face with the contents of the bucket of paint. As he reeled backwards I cleared a path through the others by the simple expedient of twirling the brush around me like a man-at-arms with a broadsword. Spot and Tiffy followed me at a safe distance and we rapidly reached the street and continued on our way. I thoughtfully handed the brush to the doorman, so that nobody stole it. It was as we walked briskly down the street, Tiffy commented thoughtfully, "My mother told me that working with you would be both interesting and educational. I thought at the time she meant it might improve my understanding of poetry."

The meal, as usual with the Great Gusto, was excellent. When, over the dessert, we did discuss Thela's comments, I confess I wasn't initially surprised. To sum them up briefly, it appeared to Thela that Sister Alanette and Maljie were engaged in a metaphorical wrestling match that had innocent bystanders running for cover. Whilst Maljie was trying to convince Sister Alanette that she could achieve much more if she became patriarch, Sister Alanette was obviously trying to convince Maljie that Maljie was the obvious person to be patriarch, because then she would be able to do so much good by prioritising the really worthwhile projects, like Sister Alanette's. The two patriarchs, watching these two ladies facing off against each other, had refused point blank to get involved. But then I'm sure you, dear reader, could have predicted those developments for yourself. What did surprise me, and simultaneously made things even more complicated, was the fact that Battass Droom had managed to catch up with Falan far more quickly than anybody expected. He had sent a note by special messenger to say that Falan didn't want to be patriarch, and that Droom himself expected to be back in Port Naain in the next two days. He also commented in his letter that he would soon have his report ready about the forged letter but wanted to combine it with an investigation into the demonic attack on the Office of the Combined Hierophants of Aea.

This latter news did perturb me. Still at times like this only a fool would rush to action. I decided I ought to contemplate my next move. This I did over a rather nice selection of cheeses and some excellent coffee. Tiffy and I agreed that it was obvious that I ought to go to the shrine to discuss matters with the others. Tiffy, interested in what might happen next, summoned a two-seater sedan chair and we made the journey in fine style.

When we dismounted at Exegesis Square I was surprised to discover how busy it was. The Deacon was using the last of the daylight to oversee the dismantling of the style. The ship's mast had already been hidden. (Where, I hear you ask, do you hide a full ship's mast? I confess I was never informed.) The platform had already been dissembled, now the base was being taken apart and the wood carried carefully to our stockpile. There it was mixed in with the other timber that our Deacon had accumulated. Frankly, given the size of the pile, the mast might even have been tucked in there somewhere.

Both patriarchs were watching and I went to join them. "What's this about Droom wanting to

investigate a demonic attack? What demonic attack?"
Sydna said, "Well when you have chanting prophets cursing a building with the full cursing ritual and then it is swamped with foul substances, a demonic attack cannot be ruled out."

Telbat commented, "Admittedly it wasn't my first thought, but I can see how a certain cast of mind would lead a person to assume that is what happened. At the same time a somewhat different cast of mind might well claim to believe it if it suited their purpose."

"So Droom will get to interview our prophet?"

"Prophet Weldun has gone into silent retreat at the Shrine of Aea the Blessed on the coast not far from Candleman's Cove."

I know the shrine, it is on the coast, with superb views and it boasts of its tranquillity, ideal for a silent retreat. It also has a reputation for culinary excellence, plus its own, outstanding, brewery. I too would welcome being sent on a silent retreat there.

Sydna added, "Apparently on the retreat he has been joined by Eddna and old Borly, among others."

I stood and watched the mendicants carefully disassembling the base. The Deacon was watching warily lest the wood be damaged. I asked, "And the stylite?"

Telbat commented, thoughtfully, "It appears he is reconsidering his vocation. The role of stylite might not be the path he is called upon to tread."

Sydna said, "We had a house painter drop in, she was looking for somebody useful with a head for heights. Our stylite decided that might be the calling he is searching for."

"I confess, I'm curious, what made him want to be a stylite in the first place?"

"The Deacon called for volunteers and I don't think the lad knew what the job entailed. I suspect it was the promise of three meals a day and a chance to snooze in the sun that sold it to him."

"And the house painter was both young and pretty." Telbat added.

It struck me that we were being diverted from the important business at hand. "So when Battass Droom arrives what happens?"

Telbat said, "Well I asked him to investigate the business of the forged signature. So it would be distinctly uncharitable not to hear his report. I think we both look forward with some interest to see what he has to say about the demonic attack. Then we have to find something to keep him busy until the remarkable Clogchipper sisters produce their report on his finances for me."

Chapter 17

The arrival of Archhierophant Battass Droom to the shrine was marked with considerable formality. As was fitting under the circumstances he was led into the main hall. At that time of day the light streaming in through the clerestory does make it particularly effective. He was escorted by all the temple wardens marching in procession, two before him, two behind him and with supernumeraries tagging along behind. I confess it looked rather like a prisoner with his escort, but that is how the order has always done it. Because it was a formal occasion, the Autocephalous Patriarch would be seated on a chair which looks remarkably like a throne on the low dais. In this case we had two patriarchs, which is something that doesn't happen every generation. Thus we'd had to go round scrounging suitable seating for them. Also we'd got a third chair of similar size and grandeur for our incumbent. We also checked various of the canons of the order, and they are remarkably vague as to matters of precedence. Instead the two patriarchs decided that they would sit the incumbent in the middle with one of them on either side. There were a number of mendicants and others sitting on the bench seats which had been pushed against the wall.

When Droom entered there was a considerable amount of bowing and similar, but then the three on the dais took their seats, the escort faded away to stand at the four cardinal points and Droom was left in the middle. We'd had a discussion about whether he should stand or have a seat. Maljie pointed out that if he were standing he could pace around whilst talking and he would tend to dominate the room. So we put a chair out for him. It was the least grand of those we had borrowed. When he sat in the chair he was forced to look up at those on the dais.

Our incumbent spoke first. "The patriarchs have asked me to chair this meeting. Apparently you have discovered who forged the letter of resignation."

"Yes, Madam. I believe I have. Whilst I have not been able to lay hold of the culprit and question them directly, the evidence points to one Filby Jallow. He works in the Office of the Combined Hierophants of Aea."

I looked across at Tiffy, given she knew Filby from work I wondered what she thought of this revelation. Her face was impassive and her hand rested lightly on Spot's collar. That intrigued me, impassive ladies tend to know far more than they are willing to reveal.

The incumbent asked, "And you have arranged for this individual to be arrested?"

"I sent word ahead for him to be arrested this morning when he came in to work. But it appears somebody may have talked. He never came into work today and he is not at his lodgings."

"You mentioned," and here the incumbent ostentatiously glanced at a piece of paper. "A demonic attack on the Office of the Combined Hierophants of Aea."

It was nicely done. Whilst there was a hint of disbelief in the tone of her voice, it wasn't enough for him to claim he had been insulted.

"This is difficult to believe but I feel that the evidence points in that direction. When you have four of the more heretical prophets making frenzied predictions, this sort of thing can happen even if it had not been planned in advance. I suspect they may have breached, or at least weakened, the empyrean barrier, perhaps accidentally. Still whatever they did was enough to allow a major diabolic expression."

The incumbent asked, "What did this diabolic expression consist of. You must remember we were out of the city at the time."

"There was some doubt. I interviewed Jaysen the night soil collector and he seemed to think it was a considerable quantity of night soil."

"I suppose one would be wise to accept his assessment in this matter. There are few better placed to make such a judgement."

At this point Sydna the hegumen asked, "I confess it is not my field, but are demonic forces in the habit of manifesting in the form of night soil? My reading of the Greater Brevity is that one should be on the lookout for foul odours, unexplained manic laughter and capering imps."

Somewhat dryly Droom commented, "I can personally vouch for the foul odour."

He pulled a book from the satchel he carried. "If I may, I shall quote from 'The life of Mottan Pye.' He was Archhierophant of Aea Undivided and he was accosted on Slip Pile Lane by a demon, in daylight, perhaps five hundred years ago."

Sydna nodded. "Read on please."

Droom had a good voice for this, he read well and with enough feeling to lift the text. It was obvious that the words were those of Mottan Pye himself.

"It was as I walked down Slip Pile Lane that the creature manifested itself. The first sign was a stench, but then the entire lane was showered in ordure, as if the privies of the city were being emptied upon us. So I turned and I met the demon with a stout heart and recited the six rituals of banishment.

Then, strong in the faith, I abjured it, spurned it and rejected it. Finally I struck it repeatedly with my staff until it fled."

Telbat the patriarch commented, "We could do with more like him."

Droom nodded. "I agree entirely. But as you see, the literature shows that showers of ordure in considerable quantities are also a sign of the demonic."

Our incumbent asked, "So what do you propose as a next step."

"Obviously we must investigate further. It is obvious we have been too lax and things have been festering." His voice grew stronger, he stood up and turned to include those watching. "For too long we have turned a blind eye to the antics of our prophets. The prophet known as Borly has long been tainted with associations of the demonic. He was present at the summoning. The prophet Eddna was present after the manifestation and was cavorting in a most unseemly manner on the scene."

The incumbent cut him off. "You have made allegations, serious allegations, but you have not answered the question. "What do you propose as the next step?"

"The prophets must be questioned."

"The prophets are currently in silent retreat at the Shrine of Aea the Blessed."

"The retreat is a sham and should be broken up."

"Silence, I know those who are leading this retreat. I will not have them traduced." Telbat was on his feet and looked genuinely angry. "If you have no evidence then stop bandying about allegations."

"I will have evidence and then we will cleanse the order. I note that your prophet was one of those involved in this foul deed."

The incumbent laid a hand on Telbat's arm. "I think Sydna wishes to speak."

Telbat sat down, still glaring at Droom.

Sydna spoke, his voice seemed quiet after the other

two. "I suspect that the Archhierophant may not be fully informed. The person leading the retreat is Sister Sassan. Telbat and I have known her for many years, indeed she trained with us, far too many years ago. In two days I have been asked to lead a meditation at the retreat. I suggest the Archhierophant accompanies me. He can join the retreat. At the very least he will get to keep an eye on the people he suspects."

"I'm not sure it is a good use of my time." Droom seemed surprised at the proposal.

"Between ourselves, Archhierophant, I would jump at the chance. When was your last retreat?" Our incumbent sounded concerned.

Droom was thrown off-balance by this approach, "I'm not sure how this is relevant."

"Because you're supposed to be a spiritual leader, not an administrative officer." Telbat had recovered from his outburst. "Too many of our hierophants forget this and it's up to their superiors to set an example. I suggest you go with Sydna here. Then take part in the retreat. At the end of the retreat you will have had time for yourself, which is rare enough, but also will have been able to observe people. Then when you come back, if you still wish to make these allegations, we will discuss them seriously and progress matters."

In his quiet way, Sydna asked, "I assume this is all settled? The Archhierophant and I will walk together to the Shrine of Aea Reimagined this evening. That should give us a full day to walk the rest of the way to the Shrine of Aea the Blessed."

Droom relaxed slightly in his chair. Perhaps he realised that he was being offered a rare chance to spend a lot of time in uninterrupted conversation with the one who could be the next Autocephalous Patriarch. "I accept your kind offer."

📖📖📖

I'd barely got back to the barge when a footman

arrived with a note, inviting Shena and myself to dine with Mortimar and Tiffy Weldonnan and a very few selected guests that evening. This was somewhat unexpected. Shena scanned the invitation and pointed to the brief, 'dress informal' note at the bottom of the note. "I suspect your friend Tiffy is intending to concentrate on more than just food and wine."

That gelled with my thinking as well. Still, given that when dressing informally, Shena is normally barefoot with her skirt hitched up as she goes out on the sands, whilst I have been known to wrestle with verse in my shirt sleeves with no collar, we decided that we would abjure excessive informality and merely turn up dressed as respectably as our wardrobes allowed. I wore the better jacket with some almost new britches. Shena had a dress in green which had only been repurposed and refreshed twice. Tiffy had a chair come and collect us which we felt was a nice touch.

When we arrived we were shown into a small side parlour. There Mortimar plied us all with drinks and through a partially open door we could see Tiffy overseeing the overloading of a buffet table. We were the last of the guests to arrive, Maljie and her sister Margarita were already present, as was Laxey; along with a somewhat bemused Brassnet, somehow looking younger and more vulnerable when he was no longer ensconced within the Office of the Combined Hierophants. Eventually Madam Tiffy joined us. She was accompanied by her daughter, Mistress Tiffy who had Spot to one side of her and Filby Jallow on the other. It struck me that both Spot and Filby were walking obediently to heel.

Madam Tiffy started by introducing Filby. It struck me that only Brassnet and I had ever met him, to the others he was just a name.

Maljie, as tactful as ever asked, "So you are the forger."

"Yes Mam."

This rather stumped her. Then Filby turned to Brassnet. "Could you explain please?"

Brassnet coughed and took a sip of his red wine. "I suppose I ought to. You see, Filby isn't really a forger, he's the 'corrections clerk.' Correcting documents is part of his job."

This struck me as odd. It was obvious that Old Mortimar hadn't been brought up to date with what was going on either. "You mean the order pays him to forge documents for them?"

"After a fashion. The problem is that most priests and others are very casual with documents. They are forever losing them. Also our office isn't very efficient, there are vast amounts of paper to store and we haven't got many staff and those we have are not particularly well remunerated. Few stay with us for any length of time."

Mistress Tiffy said, with feeling, "That I can understand. And the systems; incumbents arranged by date of ordination. It is a nightmare."

"Well I confess that that was my idea." Brassnet looked embarrassed. "It became obvious that if the system was too simple, it would be obvious how much lost and misplaced documentation there was."

Mortimar still had his teeth into the counterfeiting of documents. "But where does forging stuff come into this?"

"Ah, yes. What you have to remember is that a lot of documents are very similar. So a formal ordination report, a request for the relief from a liturgy, the annual statistics, all have largely the same format. So when we are asked to find a document and cannot find it, then it is easy enough for the corrections clerk to create a new one which says what the old one would have said."

"Including the annual statistics?"

"Well if possible the clerk would look to see what the statistics for other years were and work from them. But in all candour, nobody ever checks the numbers and we've never had anybody query what we sent them."

Maljie asked, "But this is rather different from forging a letter of resignation."

Filby said, "Not really. All that happened was Droom asked for a copy of it. He was very apologetic, saying he'd misplaced the copy we'd sent him so could we send him another copy. Most senior clergy do this, they're forever losing documents. But then we couldn't find it, which is hardly unprecedented. So we asked him what he remembered it saying and I used that to create the letter for him. Then we put the 'real' one in the file and my colleague Glenan made a copy of that, but in his own hand, unsigned, and it is stamped 'copy'. That copy we sent to Droom."

"Do you do all the corrections?"

"Not really, Maljie, I do the routine stuff. If there are deeds or similar that need correcting then, depending on age and complexity, we might get a professional in."

I was intrigued. "What about our deaths register?"

"Too much work." Filby was almost apologetic. "It would be written in a score of different hands and have far too much detail that we couldn't bluff. If we lost one of them the only way out would be for us to just deny all knowledge of it."

Mortimar was obviously struggling with this. "But how long has this been going on?"

Filby just shrugged. Brassnet said, "Well looking through the records, we've had corrections clerks for at least two hundred years."

"Provided those records haven't been 'corrected'." Mortimar muttered.

Margarita interrupted. "This is interesting no doubt, but I assume we're supposed to do something about it, or why have we been invited?"

"You mean other than for your sparkling company, wit and erudition?"

Margarita stuck her tongue out at Madam Tiffy.

Mistress Tiffy said, "Filby had to flee."

Margarita muttered, "Not very far."

Filby felt he ought to put his side of the story. "Droom told me to disappear for a few months until it all blew over. But without my salary I cannot pay my rent, and my fear is that somebody might take steps to make my disappearance permanent."

"The answer is obvious," Maljie said brightly. "Come and be one of our mendicants for a while."

Between ourselves I wasn't sure if that was a good idea. I felt that giving Maljie a corrections clerk of her own was the route to certain trouble.

Mortimar may have been thinking on similar lines. "I suggest I just take him on as a clerk in the office. One more is neither here nor there, and I can pay him a salary and he can afford to live."

Madam Tiffy stood up. "That's excellent, with everything sorted we can go through to the buffet."

Her daughter said, "There is one more thing you were going to tell them, isn't there Filby."

"Yes, a couple of weeks ago the patriarch sent me a message. He wanted details of Maljie's ordination. I checked and there were no details for her, not even a cubby hole. So I found a gap."

"A gap?"

"Yes, Madam Tiffy. Basically somebody had died and we'd not yet cleaned out their cubby hole. So all I did was copy that person's ordination document, complete with the signature of the Archhierophant presiding, only with Maljie's name on it. So Maljie's lost ordination has been recovered and everything is legal once again."

Maljie managed to say, "But I've never been ordained."

"You were, about fifteen years ago."

Margarita managed to say, "Which means you've got plenty of seniority when they want to appoint you patriarch. With that she collapsed into helpless laughter.

Chapter 18

It is surprising how quickly the Grand Slide came round. Much to my dismay I discovered that apparently I was the only person who could arrange things. So whilst the wise sat on committees and debated matters of import, they left the sordid business of organising the details to me. Here I was fortunate in that Almas Slackwater also threw herself into the project. Maljie would occasionally make an appearance but she was still engaged in her battle of wills with Sister Alanette. My cousin Thela told me that she was watching Maljie and Sister Alanette work together. She had come to the conclusion that the two ladies genuinely liked and respected each other, but were not going to let the other inveigle them into becoming the next Patriarch. Thela also commented that it was only a matter of time before they combined to inflict the role on somebody else. She warned me to avoid meeting both ladies at the same time, and whilst I wasn't sure whether she was joking or not, it struck me as entirely good advice. Indeed I even dropped round to the Office of the Combined Hierophants to check that I hadn't been retrospectively ordained.

We formed a subcommittee of three in the barge, Almas and I, with Shena acting as the voice of reason. It was decided in the interests of practicality that whilst the event would start at the Council of Sinecurists building, it would head along Sinecurists Walk, turn into New Gallows Prospect and finally plunge down Lame Pauper's Ginnel. The finishing line would be on Ropewalk.

Early on we fixed the design of the vehicle to that which the Deacon had sketched out. A shortage of decent wheels in the city meant we had to approve a second design with cast iron wheels.

They were cheaper if nothing else. We fixed the 'crew' of the vehicle to two. There was a children's day when, frankly they could go down on anything they wanted. We decided that there would be an event for husbands and wives. In the interests of finance, we also agreed that there would be another day for those cases where a lady used her chair men or similar. We hoped that this would encourage the sedan chair racing sisterhood to take part. After all, they would happily pay an entrance fee and they'd also bring in the bookmakers. Finally there would be the open section where you could use your own design of vehicle and crew numbers.

As the day drew near I requisitioned the literate mendicants and had them making lists of those who wished to compete. Maljie, Laxey and I walked the course and decided which roads crossing our route would have to be blocked off to prevent accidents. Thespan Slackwater as Master of the Snows organised it, and, a nice touch this, arranged that the roads be blocked off using stands which allowed spectators a view of the spectacle. A small but not unreasonable fee was charged for entry to these stands.

All in all everything was organised entirely competently. I'd even thought to have a small platform built out of beer barrels with a couple of old doors laid across it. I could stand on that with a small table on which to rest my paperwork. It meant I could see over the heads of the throng, and people could find me. Whilst the latter isn't always an entirely good thing, at times like this I tend to break my rule of graceful semi-anonymity. It also spares me having to listen to people bellowing, 'Where is that idiot Steelyard hiding.'

I also had one stroke of good luck, the Widow Handwill volunteered to help. Almas Slackwater hoped to compete and had been looking for somebody who could assist me. The Widow was, as always, a joy to work with. Not only is she great fun, but with the children, she was the grandmother they instinctively turned to.

When it came to the married couples, everybody knew that had her husband lived, she would have been an enthusiastic participant. As for the 'semi-professional' racers on the third day, the Widow knew everybody. After all she had been a leading light in sedan chair racing circles. Unfortunately for her, her daughters and assorted grandchildren had impressed upon her that she was to behave as befitted a lady of her age and have no part in these wild antics. They relented enough to agree that she could take part in an administrative capacity.

The first day was the children's races. Because we didn't burden them with strict rules regarding the design of their chosen vehicles there was a fine array of imaginative constructions. As an aside I believe I solved the hitherto unexplained mystery of the city wide phenomenon of disappearing wheelbarrows. The number of spectators was higher than I had expected. I would have predicted a good turnout of mothers, aunts, doting grandparents, members of the watch hoping to pick up the usual suspects. As it was we got a lot of adult contestants who seemed to be casting a professional eye over how the course ran and what tactics worked best. All in all it was a good day, meat pie sellers and similar commented to me that they'd had an excellent trade, as had the impromptu bar set up by the simple expedient of selling the beer from the back of a dray. If asked to run a comparable event I'd be tempted to increase the rent they were charged for their pitches.

Listening to the talk, it seemed that there were two approved tactics. If you had a light outfit then the obvious way to proceed was to pull it as fast as possible to the top of Lame Pauper's Ginnel, then jump aboard and hope you had the velocity to keep your lead all the way to the bottom.

If, on the other hand, you had a heavier contraption, you were never going to be first to the top of the steep descent, but once on that descent your speed would be eye watering.

Provided you could steer your contraption adequately you should be able to overtake lighter vehicles. Given the uncertain nature of some of the steering mechanisms, pushing the opposition into the walls as you went past seemed to be regarded as a reasonable alternative.

Given the number of competitors, we ran several heats during the day, and the day finished with the final. This was run off between the victors of the heats. I felt that this was a fair way of arranging matters and it meant that those with the more robust vehicle had an advantage. So in one case, the winner of one heat did indeed come first. One wag pointed out they came first, second, and fourth. The front wheels arrived first, bouncing down the slope, with spectators fleeing out of their path. Then came the competitors, their contrivance now a sledge rather than a cart. They were followed by the next competitor whose vehicle had held together rather better, followed by the winner's rear wheels.

The second day was, I hoped, going to be more genteel. Unfortunately I had forgotten to allow for the rivalries and competitiveness among married ladies. The bookmakers had, metaphorically, got their eye in and were able to give considered odds. As all competitors were using carts of standard design attention focussed on those who were riding on the carts. So the slim lady with the muscular husband was well favoured. The large lady with the smaller husband less so. In reality things were more complicated. It appears that the large lady had wisely added considerable padding so she was not as large as she appeared. Similarly her husband was remarkably fit for a man of his age. He managed to keep up with the favourite and at the top of Lame Pauper's Ginnel both husbands leapt aboard the back of the carts at almost the same time.

It was now the larger lady showed her mettle. Whether her morale was boosted by the padding, but frankly she was without fear.

At one point spectators marvelled at the showers of sparks thrown up as her cast iron wheels scraped along the wall as she got past an early leader on the inside. Whilst it may have pained the bookies, she was a popular winner with the spectators.

The third day was one for the aficionado. The competition was fierce, the participants had had two days to learn from the mistakes of others, and none of them were willing to take prisoners. I remember a lot of very tight finishes with three heats having to be rerun because the first two across the line were too close to call.

One the fourth day, I rather relaxed. This was the day for eccentrics, inventors, dilettantes and dabblers. I could not imagine people getting too over-excited and races ending up in fisticuffs. The first heat proved me wrong. The competitors had been chosen at random, and the first heat involved five comparatively low slung machines and one that looked if it had been designed by the gentleman's coachman. The inventor had taken advantage of the flexibility in the rules and had a score of men pulling using ropes. At the top of the incline they would all dive into the coach and career down the hill at speed. Now large heavy vehicles often struggled to get to the top of Lame Pauper's Ginnel first. Here, because of the number of men with ropes, they achieved this quite easily by spreading out and blocking the road so that rather than a race, it resembled a procession. Admittedly a procession moving with more speed than dignity, but still a procession.

Once on the downhill the coach driver was obviously confident in his size and weight. The contrivance had evidently been measured as it was too wide to overtake.

At this point my admiration for the ingenuity of my fellow citizens bursts forth.

          Such genius would beg
              A triumph
          Award a baccalaureate.
              A wooden leg
          (Let the critics harrumph)
  Through the spokes of the triumphal chariot.

Indeed Swale Higginspot it was who overcame the
obstruction. An inveterate inventor, he had suffered
his fair share of injuries in the sundry explosions and
collisions of the past. Thus he steered his low slung
vehicle, whilst a younger and fitter companion
pushed. When he caught up with the coach he
grasped the problem, and unfastened his wooden leg
and jammed it between the spokes of a rear wheel.
The coach juddered to an abrupt halt with a shattered
wheel and Swale and his companion shot under it and
took the lead. The rest of the pack followed his lead
and the monstrosity was left to be dragged down the
hill by the men with ropes.
At the bottom the atmosphere of cheery good-
fellowship we had tried to engender dissipated rapidly
and the resulting brawl was only broken up when
spectators joined in to rescue Swale who was trapped
in his immobile vehicle, forced to defend himself with
a crutch of his own devising.
In the penultimate event, Almas Slackwater and her
younger sister took part. They managed to avoid the
whole sweaty business of pushing their vehicle by the
simple expedient of installing clockwork which they
wound up before the start of the race. They were last
to the top of Lame Pauper's Ginnel, but the weight of
the mechanism worked in their favour and whilst they
never won their heat, they were roundly applauded.
The two young women had gone for demure elegance
and had ridden in style wearing long, elegant, dresses
and carried parasols. There was a feeling that they
had captured the spirit of the occasion.
It was as the winners of the various heats were
gathering for the final race.

A young female mendicant appeared at the foot of my platform and said, "You staying there fer long?"
I was a little put out by this, but answered, "Well until the last race has been run and we have a winner." Then curiosity got the better of me. "Why?"
"Maljie wanted to know. Her and that Sister wants a word with you."
That didn't sound encouraging so I pigeonholed it as one of those things I could worry about when I had time.
All the finalists were now in place, each had been given a little while to ensure everything was tightened and in place. Hosiery and wheel bearings were being adjusted. The Widow Handwill was looking at a cart that had been left by my platform.
"Tallis, this one seems to be in decent working order." I have known the Widow for many years, I answered in as non-committal manner as I could manage. "Is it."
"Don't you think the race looks tremendous fun?" Now to be fair, it isn't perhaps how I would have described it. Indeed were I to write a poem on the topic I would major heavily on synonyms for 'terrifying.' Still it was at that point that I saw Trane Forsgill and a number of his friends walking towards the my position. They appeared to be carrying buckets of paint. I glanced in the opposite direction. There I saw Maljie and Sister Alanette heading towards me. I glanced once more at the cart. The other carts were taking their position in the start line. "Get on board, I'll push."
We were almost in position when the cord dropped for the race to start. The cart we had acquired was one with a bar at the back to allow the gentleman to push, rather than a rope which allowed you to pull. To be honest I thought the bar a superior method. I'd noted several gentlemen who had had to leap to one side to avoid their out-of-control carriage hurtling down on them.
Now remember that the Widow and I had not

practiced, but on the other hand the other participants had already run one race. So we were fresher but naïve. Not only that but I had excellent reasons for haste. We might have been last at the start but we were third at the top of Lame Pauper's Gill. This is where I could use the design of our cart to its full advantage, I kept pushing until the cart was nearly going faster than I was and then jumped aboard.

Some of the carts with a bar expected the gentleman to swing himself under it feet first, landing in the seat with his legs either side of the lady. Which was perfectly proper with a married couple. The system was not without problems, more than one lady had been kicked out of her car when the gentleman, panicking, hit her in the back with both feet. Our car had a ledge, I merely stepped onto it and clung to the bar for dear life.

Now it was all up to the Widow. My extra pushing had propelled us to second place. I was happy enough with this. I was more interesting in flight than winning. The Widow on the other hand has a competitive streak on these occasions. We were gaining on the cart ahead, and the cart behind was gaining on us.

It was on the first corner that we realised our vehicle had a design flaw. Because I was standing at the back, behind the back wheels, there wasn't as much weight on the front wheels as you might hope, so the steering was a little 'light.' Instead of gracefully cornering, our right front wheel scraped along the wall, showering me with brick dust and sparks. The cart behind swung left and started to overtake us on that side. The Widow shouted, "Tallis, lean forward." Our front wheels bit and she took us left to close the gap. Unfortunately our left front wheel hit the other cart's right front wheel. Cast iron bounced off cast iron. Then the other cart ricocheted off to the left, scraped along that wall and we gained on it.

We were now on the steepest section and were moving at what can only be called a ridiculous pace. I was leaning so far over the bar that my face was nearly buried in the Widow's hat. As we went into the next corner the cart in front went too far to the left and scraped along the wall slowing it down. The Widow brought us right and we started sneaking past just as the other cart came back across. Our left wheel hit their back wheel, cast iron on cast iron again, and at this point our wheel shattered. The Widow shouted, "Tallis, lean back."

I immediately hung as far back as I could off the bar and shifting my weight meant that our front wheels were barely touching the ground. In spite of only having one, we managed to keep going, but obviously steering was impossible. Still by shouting for me to throw my weight left or right, and running our broken wheel along the wall, she managed to get us round the last corner.

Unfortunately this had lost us time and the third cart was coming up behind us. The Widow drifted us to the right in an attempt to cut them up but they were too fast and our steering too tentative. We crossed the finishing line neck and neck and were awarded joint second.

We accepted the congratulations of the other participants and as things settled down I said to the Widow. "I'm going to quietly disappear. I'll join Shena on the Old Esplanade. There are too many ill-intentioned people looking for me round here."

"Can I come with you? I noticed one of my daughters was watching from the last stand we passed. When she catches up with me I'll never hear the last of it."

Chapter 19

As we sat in the barge I half listened as the Widow described our day to Shena. All the while I was pondering what to do next. Finally as the tale drew to a close I said, "I have to be at the Grand Ball this evening."

The Widow asked, "Is that the one at Madam Halgan's house."

I must have winced. Shena actually patted me gently on the arm. "I know, Mesdames Halgan and Malwin have given you sleepless nights."

"Well they both wanted to host the Grand Ball, but by definition there is only one. So one of them had to lose."

"How did you decide who was to be hostess?"

Shena said casually, "Tallis suggested they toss a coin for it."

"Which went down very badly."

Shena patted my arm again. "And then Almas suggested they wrestle naked in mud, the winner taking all."

"Maljie didn't help, bursting out laughing and suggesting that we held the naked mud wrestling instead of the Grand Slide on the grounds it would have raised far more money."

"So how did you decide?" The Widow was intrigued.

"Maljie just said, "You this year, you next year.""

"So you're doing this again?" Shena asked.

I just shrugged. "I hope that they consider some form of financial recompense."

The Widow was shocked, "They haven't paid you?"

"Not a dreg. The only money I made was on side bets. I did well on Greta Frots."

The Widow said, judiciously, "Her victory was unexpected."

"Her chairmen are twins. She used one on the first race and swapped him for the fresh one on the second."

"But Susenna Tweel had a lot better time in her heat."

"Yes, she was ahead of Greta in the final until her back axle snapped and both back wheels fell off."

"And you knew that was going to happen?"

"Well I saw Susenna having a word with 'Comeback' Hoon the bookie."

Shena called us back to the present. "You ought to get ready for the Grand Ball."

"True." I turned to the Widow. "Are you planning to attend?"

"I'm supposed to, but going home to get changed means meeting a deputation of daughters and granddaughters and I'm not looking forward to that. I wouldn't have believed how such charming and mischievous children could have grown to be such straitlaced and disapproving women."

Shena said, "Well I can lend you something."

The Widow smiled gently. "Shena, I love you as a daughter, and I know that was well meant, but I suspect that the only things you have in your wardrobe that might fit me will be shoes and a handbag."

"No, I've got several nice gowns that Tallis was given by patrons. I've not got round to repurposing them yet. I'd bet some of them might fit."

The Widow looked hopeful. "It's certainly worth a try."

The two ladies disappeared into our cabin whilst I took the opportunity to heat some water, wash and shave in the main saloon. After an hour or so Shena and the Widow emerged. Both were wearing long dresses, but short enough for dancing. Shena announced, "I knew we could do it."

The Widow gave a twirl. "It must be forty years out of date, but who cares, I might start a new fashion. Certainly the lines flatter the more mature figure." She immediately became more practical. "I will summon two chairs and we can travel in style."

At the Ball itself, I slipped off and entered via the kitchen. It wasn't merely I wanted to miss being ambushed by Maljie at the entrance (Trane Forsgill and paint carrying friends were less of an issue. I may have inadvertently upset Madam Halgan's sensitivities but not to that extent) but I really needed to check with Madam Halgan's cook that everything was going according to plan.

That worthy lady was entirely in control of the situation, and waved cheerfully at me over the heads of numerous extra kitchen porters hired for the evening. From there I went up the back stairs and met the housekeeper who showed me the small spare bedroom that had been put at my disposal as an office. This was a novelty but as I also needed somewhere to house the various prizes, it was probably wise.

I also checked the prizes. Madam Halgan had had quiet words with the parents, husbands or close friends of winners and from the budget allotted had arranged entirely suitable prizes. Thus we had a pair of puppies for the winning children's team, a crate of a rather nice wine for the couples, a bale of particularly beautiful silk for the winning 'semi-professional' and a number of classic engineering tomes for the winner of the open section. Having seen his contrivance in operation I really hoped he'd study them.

Then I went down to the ballroom. Here I felt I was safe. Even Maljie was not going to bellow, 'Steelyard, you're to be Patriarch' across the dance floor at me. As it was she and Sister Alanette sat together at one of the tables. They were watching me with the casual confidence of predators secure in the knowledge that their prey is trapped.

There was the usual meeting and greeting of people, admiring black eyes and obvious contusions and signing casts.

The last time I attended a ball where so many of the guests of honour were barely able to walk because of their injuries was in Partann of all places!

About half an hour before the prize giving I decided I'd better nip back to 'my office' and check the prizes. I was a little wary about unaccompanied puppies, even if they were confined. When I arrived I found them dozing peacefully with no signs of wreckage. I decided that I'd take the opportunity to jot down a few ideas that had occurred to me with regards my impromptu remarks. So I sat at the table, took out my indelible pencil and suddenly there was a hullaballoo outside. I did the obvious thing, I made my way to the door and locked it. The door looked comfortingly heavy and there were three bolts. As I listened it was obvious that the noise was along the corridor a little so I risked opening my door slightly and looking out. There were half a dozen burly individuals around the next door. One of them I recognised. It was Gervas Filportal. He was hammering on the door and shouting about adulterers and betrayal. Given he maintains three mistresses to my certain knowledge I felt he was wise majoring on a topic he knew so well. I quietly closed the door and bolted it. I turned to walk back to the desk and realised somebody was attempting to open my window. This was a full length glass door which opened onto a balcony. I picked up a poker from the fireplace and opened the window. There was a man wearing only a robe with a cowl that hid his face. He burst past me and said, "Rescue the lady."

I stepped out onto the balcony. There was another balcony on which the lady stood. She was frenziedly attempting to put her clothes on. Whilst her gentleman admirer had managed to jump to my balcony, it was a feat I would not have wanted to emulate. I went back into my room, took a sheet from the bed, tied it to the balcony rail and climbed the short distance to the ground.

I then ran round to the back door where the sedan chair bearers were waiting. I found a chair with a good solid roof (I hate those with only light canvas tops. Yes I know they're faster but still) and summoned the bearers. They followed me at a jog, held their chair by the balcony and when the lady stepped onto the roof they lowered the chair to the ground and I handed her down and into the chair. It was Madam Filportal. I turned to the bearers, "Take the lady to the Shrine to Aea in her Aspect as the Personification of Tempered Enthusiasm, she will pay."

I then clambered up to my balcony and the gentleman I had assisted, now fully dressed, and helped me back onto it. It was Philiman, the theologically sanctioned beggar.

From next door came the sound of a crash. It sounded like Gervas Filportal and his followers had smashed the door down. I looked at Philiman with his robes and sandals. "Right, you're my mendicant assistant. Grab the two puppies and the wine, I'll take the silk and the books. Follow me, say nothing and keep your head down."

We walked out of the room and down the corridor. Filportal and his minions were standing in the smashed doorway, arguing with the butler and housekeeper. I blessed the brisk efficiency of Madam Halgan's household. I've worked in houses where the domestic staff didn't notice when builders took down a wing by mistake. On seeing me arrive Madam Halgan called the dancers to order and her maids shepherded the prize winners into position.

Things went remarkably well. Maljie gave a short talk about the amount of money raised. Sister Alanette then announced that she was about to start purchasing the property she needed. Then the prize giving proper started. Maljie and Sister Alanette shook hands or kissed the prize winners.

Philiman would hand the prize to Sister Alanette who would give it to the worthy recipient.

With the puppies he just set them down on the ground and the puppies each chose their delighted new owner. Then before the two ladies could recall my presence to mind and find a quiet moment, I faded quietly away, taking Philiman with me.

We walked to the shrine, and as we walked I asked the obvious question. "Philiman, you are somebody who is known for his high standards, indeed you're known for living a moral life, not just lecturing on it. Yet I have to rescue you from an aggrieved husband."

"It's a long story."

"It's a fair walk as well, so take your time."

"Well Neila Filportal and I want to marry. But her husband won't give her a divorce."

"He cannot stop her. She just has to put a formal request to the Council of Sinecurists and if her request remains on their books for a twelve month, they'll automatically nod through the divorce."

"Yes, but their marriage was celebrated in a Shrine of Aea, and so the Council have no say in the matter."

I could see where he was coming from. With marriages solemnised by a priest of Aea, divorce is possible but only if both ask for it. "And Gervas doesn't want a divorce?" To be honest that surprised me.

"He's not shared a bed with her for six years, but if he divorces her he has to move out of her house."

I could see the problem. "Can you not get somebody from the order to annul the marriage? It can be done, surely." This was one of those areas temple wardens rarely venture into. It isn't the sort of thing that we're expected to deal with.

"The only person who can annul a marriage if one of the parties doesn't want it annulled is the Autocephalous Patriarch."

"I have the glimmerings of an idea."

We walked in silence. On arrival at the shrine I took Philiman to meet Neila. It was then I put my idea to them.

"Neila, I assume you want to marry this man?"

"Yes."

Well there was no equivocation there.

"And you, Philiman, want to marry Neila?"

"Yes."

"Right, the way forward is simple. The only person who can annul Neila's marriage is the Autocephalous Patriarch. So you will have to become Patriarch. Then you can annul the marriage and then marry her yourself."

Neila asked, "Can that be done."

"With no difficulty whatsoever."

Neila hugged Philiman. "Then arrange it."

I led the loving couple into the library where our two patriarchs were sitting in conversation.

"Gentlemen, Philiman, our theologically sanctioned beggar has volunteered to become Patriarch.

Telbat stood up and shook his hand. "An excellent decision." With this he turned to Sydna. "I heartily recommend him. He's theologically sound, modest in his habits, knows all the routines, and will do an excellent job."

Sydna also stood up and shook the hand of their bemused successor. "Is it wise for me to ask what Tallis promised you to get you to agree to do the job?"

Neila spoke rapidly. "Tallis said that when Philiman becomes patriarch, he can dissolve my marriage and then we can marry."

"It's true. Her husband refuses her a divorce even though he's had nothing to do with her for six or more years."

Sydna relaxed slightly. "That is no problem at all. Knowing our good poet I feared we were condemned to publishing several slim volumes of undoubtedly worthy poetry."

It struck me that I had perhaps been slow here. But even as I pondered my own failings, Telbat added, "No problem whatsoever. Although whilst a Patriarch can marry, he cannot actually conduct his own service.

So once you're ready, perhaps Sydna and I could do it."

Neila blushed, "Can you do it soon?"

Telbat smiled, "Madam, I want to cross the mountains whilst it's still summer, if it's anything to do with me you'll be married by the end of the week."

I left them having a celebratory drink and discussing timings. It occurred to me that if Philiman was suitably grateful, he might well be inveigled into having his office fund the publication of some poems I had been working on. Still it was growing late and I wanted to get back to the ball. As it was, I got to the door of the shrine in time to meet Maljie and Sister Alanette entering. The two ladies took an arm each, and Maljie said. "Tallis, we've been trying to have a word with you in private. We have decided that you'd make an excellent patriarch."

I tried to look downcast, but probably didn't succeed. "I'm sorry to inform you that there is no longer a vacancy. We have a volunteer who is acceptable to the other two."

Gently I disengaged myself. "Anyway I must be going, it's getting late and I have to collect my lady wife from the Ball. Who knows, if I make haste I might even get there in time to have a dance with her."

Chapter 20

It was next morning when I was awakened by somebody hammering on the door of the barge. Somewhat wearily I dressed and made my way to the door. The hammering ceased as the hammerer heard me slide the bolt. As I cautiously opened the door, one of the less socially inhibited mendicants glared at me. "Bout bluidy time. Some of us 'as work to get on wi'. You're wanted at the Shine at noon."

I was struggling to cope with this. "You woke me to tell me about a noon meeting?"

"It's damned near noon now. I must 'ave bin 'ammering for hours."

I glanced at the sun, or rather the vague glow in the cloud which indicated where it might be. By my reckoning there must be at least an hour to noon.

"You said you had work to do."

"Yeh."

"Then go and do it."

With that I slammed the door shut and winced at the noise. Shena had already got the stove going and was heating water. We sat in silence until I had made coffee.

📖📖📖

As it was, I arrived at the shrine just before noon and was shown into our library. The three 'patriarchs' were sitting at the table, along with our incumbent and the rest of the shrine's leading lights. Laxey passed me coffee as I came in. It was Telbat who called the meeting to order.

"Tomorrow we have arranged for all who are in the area to attend an emergency conclave. It will be held here. We will announce that we have chosen a new patriarch, Philiman. But first we have matters that must be dealt with. We have been studying the Clogchippers' report." That certainly ensured we all sat up and took notice. "Marisol commented that she'd never seen a set of accounts as nicely put together or as accurate."

Well that wasn't quite what we'd expected to hear. Sydna said quietly, "Stop teasing them."

Telbat continued. "The accounts are in effect the books of a loan fund. They list loans made to people and institutions within the order. The loans, whilst carefully documented, were all interest free and if there was difficulty repaying the loan was extended and in some cases, increased. So the expenditure is to the nearest dreg, all very carefully itemised. What is somewhat less clear is the income.

Whilst money is marked as coming into the account, it is never mentioned where it comes from. At times you can link repayments of loans to income coming into the fund, but most is introduced from outside."

Philiman asked, "Why was he doing it?"

"I compared the list of his debtors with the twenty-three proxy votes he had gathered to support Sydna here. Whilst he loaned money to people who didn't give him their proxy vote, all the twenty-three owed him considerable sums."

Our incumbent asked, "What were they doing with the money?"

"That the Clogchippers were not asked to investigate, but I note that two shrines used their loans for major roof repairs, some of the others also did various useful things with it. I have no doubt that others invested it wisely in strong drink, slow horses and fast women."

Philiman said thoughtfully, "I hope you two are going to deal with this matter before you leave office rather than dumping it in my lap."

"The temptation was there," Sydna admitted. "But we've come up with a solution. We've also invited Droom to meet with us here." He turned to Maljie. "Would you be so kind as to see if he's arrived and bring him in if he has."

In less than five minutes, Maljie returned, followed by Droom. It was as Maljie sat down that he realised there wasn't a chair for him. He stood, slightly undecided, and Telbat said, "We've been through your accounts. You've been lending considerable sums, but we are less well informed as to where the money came from."

I confess that I was impressed by Droom at this point. Calmly he replied, "In an organisation like the order, it is surprising how much money falls between the cracks. Also there are a lot of 'inducements' to ensure that people get contracts. I took the inducements but unlike my predecessors I didn't spend them on personal luxury."

Telbat said, "I did notice the source of the proxy votes."

Sydna said, "Telbat and I have been discussing matters. If you hadn't acted as you did we would have had to step in several times to rescue people from the results of their own fecklessness."

"Droom it has occurred to us that you have managed to prove that you are one of the few competent administrators the order has got."

"Thank you, Patriarchs."

Telbat continued. "We had decided to ask our successor here, Philiman, to cancel all loans within the order. Effectively people will be told that they're written off and don't owe you anything. But it struck us that it would look better coming from you."

"It would?"

"Prior to you going to spend some time in a monastery."

"Somewhere distant where I can be forgotten." Droom sounded more resigned than bitter.

"Not exactly," Sydna said. "I need a Claustral Prior. I have promised to send Father Goodwill to assist Philiman. It means Philiman has somebody loyal and competent he can rely on. But it means I need a Claustral Prior."

"And you want me?"

"Well I suspect that with Father Goodwill showing you the ropes for a month, you'll soon have everything under control. It's time we had a new broom, the Father himself keeps saying he's got stuck in his ways. Then after a few years, I suspect the Father will want to retire to a quiet shrine somewhere. You would be the obvious person to replace him. Not only that but if you weren't careful, you might find that they try and make you Patriarch at some point."

Droom looked confused. "Incumbent, could you explain to me what these two are doing?"

"I think they feel you have become side-tracked, you're too focussed on power, authority, and influence.

But given you're one of the few competent managers we have, they're trying to get you to refocus."

"After all, what's the point in plotting for power when you're probably going to get it anyway?" Philiman commented. "Trust me, by the time they want you to be Patriarch you'll be wondering whether you couldn't just slope off and doing something more interesting."

"Why are you doing it?" Droom asked, suddenly curious.

"I'm marrying into the job. So for me the price is well worth paying. I hope you agree to the plan because I don't want to be trapped in this job forever looking for a successor."

Droom turned to Sydna. "I would be delighted to apply for the position of your Claustral Prior. I suspect it will be a valuable learning experience for me. I may one day learn to be devious enough to be a patriarch."

Synda said, "I have every confidence in your abilities."

📖📖📖

The emergency conclave went well. The two patriarchs announced they'd chosen Philiman, and everybody congratulated them on their wisdom. The assembled clerics raised him up carried him shoulder high around the outside of the shrine. Then he was sworn in. That done, for his first formal action he called for Gervas and Neila Filportal to appear in front of him. Now Neila was present, but we needed Gervas.

I suppose we could just have invited him, but before the conclave had even started Maljie and I, as temple wardens, had gone to collect him. We'd had a couple of the younger mendicants watching him so we knew where to find him. He was in his office.

One of the mendicants, dressed in conventional street clothes for the purpose, went into the office and asked if there was a reward for telling Filportal where his wife and her fancy man were hiding. Filportal thrust some coins into the outstretched hand and rushed out of the building. In the doorway he tripped over the churchwarden's wands Maljie and I stuck out in his path and before he had recovered, half a dozen of our most muscular mendicants had gagged him, bound him hand and foot, wrapped him in a length of carpet and were carrying him on their shoulders back to the shrine.

In retrospect it might have been an overreaction on our part, but it saved a lot of time, and meant he didn't embarrass himself getting on the wrong side of the Autocephalous Patriarch.

When Philiman commanded the presence of the Filportals, Neila stepped forward and Gervas, now unbound, was also thrust in front of the conclave. Maljie and I stood on either side of him.

"Do you wish for a divorce?"

Neila said simply, "Yes."

Gervas shouted, 'No'.

Philiman asked Neila, "Your reasons?"

"Adultery and neglect."

I stepped forward. "I have here a list of his mistresses. There are nine names on the list and we have five of the ladies waiting outside to testify." This was the easiest part of my job. It took me two brief conversations to come up with the names of his mistresses, and most of them, when approached, were happy to testify. Never underestimate the anger of an ex-mistress.

Philiman turned to Gervas. "Do you want this to proceed?"

"Yes, I'll fight it."

Philiman smiled a big beautiful smile. "Alas, in this case, I have absolute authority. I am convinced that your marriage is over, therefore by the authority you granted me when you married under the auspices of Aea, I dissolve entirely the marriage. You are no longer man and wife."

He looked round, "Where is the corrections clerk please?"

Filby came forward, with the original marriage certificate.

"Thank you Filby. Could you please cancel the original certificate and fill in the appropriate documents for each of them."

Gervas looked as if he were about to say something. Maljie stood firmly on his foot and whispered in his ear, "Please cause trouble, please."

⫷⫷⫷

I have organised weddings, but only for really good patrons. Frankly they are a nightmare. But to be fair to Neila, I've never worked with a more reasonable bride. Given she had two days between her divorce and her wedding, she didn't have time to panic. The service itself was formal. It has to be when a Patriarch gets married. Sydna dressed as always, in his monkish habit. Telbat surprised us, he arrived wearing the long off-white robe of a mendicant priest of Aea Undivided. After the service and the wedding breakfast, Sydna and Droom headed north with Maljie and Margarita in the latter's cart. The plan was that they could collect Maljie's Balloon. Maljie was rather hoping she could catch the end of season winds that come out of the northeast which would let her fly back. She would do this without a companion, but she hoped that Father Goodwill would have a decent quantity of class one lichen for her to transport instead.

Telbat, his staff in one hand, came up to me. "Tallis, I'm setting off. I've managed to beg deck passage on a paddler for Avitas. Then I'll join a party crossing the Slash and heading east."

"You're still going to be a priest in Tideholt then?"

"Yes, I think I was a good priest, all those years ago when they left me alone to do my job. I think I'll be a good priest again. Anyway, walk with me to the wharf."

As we walked along I asked, "I assume there was a reason you wanted to speak to me?"

"Various reasons. One was to ask you to pass on my thanks to your shrine. It is both unnerving and reassuring for a Patriarch to know you have people who are willing to do what is right, as well as what is necessary."

I was quite taken aback by that, then he continued. "Oh yes, the 'demonic attack.' I recognise night soil when I smell it. But I'm intrigued as to how it arrived there."

"A trebuchet. The style erected for the mendicant could double as a trebuchet. Apparently our deacon is somebody who worries about accuracy and detail. Hence all three cart loads just about hit the target."

"Thank you for that. I noticed that the style had disappeared."

"I overheard our deacon talking the other day. He feels that if we give him another chance he'll make an even bigger one using multiple masts laminated together. I think we talked him out of it. We pointed out that you'd need a really fat mendicant to make the whole thing convincing."

Then I asked him, "So you're serious about being a mendicant priest?"

"I've done it before and it'll do me good to do it again. Actually I suspect it's a bit similar to your trade. You have to be an interesting person and tell stories that draw people in, and they end up feeding you."

"I hope you've got plenty of good stories."

"I can tell tales of the mad patriarch and his antics. That'll keep my audience in stitches."

By this time we had reached the wharf. A paddler was waiting. It had steam up, and the crews were standing around the bottom of the gangplanks.

He held out his hand and I shook it. "Best of luck with the story telling."

"Thank you." He raised his staff slightly. "And a blessing on you, Tallis Steelyard."

With that he turned, walked up the gangplank and disappeared into the throng on the deck. I sauntered back. It struck me that it might be worth one more visit to the Office of the Combined Hierophants of Aea to check if Maljie had had me ordained. When I got there, Brassnet was walking across the entrance hall. He stopped and looked at me. "Tallis Steelyard, you may be able to help me."

"If I can…."

He beckoned me to walk with him. "It's about Eudicea."

"Eudicea?"

"Tiffy's mendicant girl, used to be called Snotty."

"Why, have you got a problem with her?"

"No problems whatsoever. But we'll have a problem is she doesn't work here. She's got Personnel running beautifully. But she isn't technically employed here. She just stayed on when Tiffy got involved elsewhere."

"So employ her."

"But we need the proper papers signed."

"Who by?"

"We need a letter of application co-signed by an ordained priest."

We walked into Personnel. Eudicea looked up from the basket of papers she was sorting. I asked, "Are you happy working here."

"Yes."

"Right, I'll deal with your letter of application. But first you'll have to get me my certificate of ordination, and also could you bring Maljie's as well."

She looked at me, then slowly disappeared into the shelving. She came back with two certificates. I studied them. Apparently I'd been an ordained priest for nearly thirty years. Indeed by chance I had allegedly been a priest longer than Maljie.

Eudicea said, "Oh we had a Father Nattan in, from Sweethaven. He wrote complaining. Twice.

Apparently the usual procedure is to ignore this sort
of letter on the grounds that having written them and
got things off their chests, those complaining forget
all about it. But this chap finally travelled down from
Sweethaven just to complain about you."

"Was he a fat man, bad tempered."

"Well he wasn't fond of you. Was most put out when I
showed him your ordination papers and you'd been a
priest longer than he had."

I wasn't sure what to say there, so I said nothing. It
looked as if Helgi's wedding was legal after all. So I
just wrote out a letter of application. Eudicea signed it
and then I signed it, perhaps for the first and only
time in my life, as 'Tallis Steelyard, Priest of Aea
Undivided.' I then added the date of my 'ordination.'
I passed the letter to Brassnet. "I assume that is
adequate?"

"Perfectly."

I folded up the two certificates and slipped them into
my jacket pocket. "I'd better look after these, I'd hate
them to fall into the wrong hands?"

"Whose hands?"

"Well, principally Maljie's."

It is entirely possible that you have enjoyed this book and fancy reading more about Tallis Steelyard, Maljie and the others.

There are three slim volumes of collected tales available.

Maljie. The Episodic Memoirs of a Lady
Maljie. Just One Thing after Another
Maljie. Teaching a Cat to Dance

Also there are a lot more stories set in Port Naain, you can find them at

https://www.amazon.co.uk/Jim-Webster/e/B009UT450I

Whilst Tallis Steelyard even has a blog available for the discerning and undiscerning alike!

https://tallissteelyard.wordpress.com/